THE HEART OF A MOTHER AND THE HAND OF GOD

∞

Bonnie Horton

XULON PRESS

Table of Contents

Dedication

I dedicate this book to the God of my salvation. It is he who has walked with me down this road of life. His mighty hand held me up and sustained me every step of the way. To him be the glory and honor for this book. I could never praise him enough for his great love for me.

I dedicate this book also to my three daughters who are with the Lord. Thank you my precious ones, for the time we shared in this life. I am thankful for the love we shared. I praise God for the promise of eternity; where we will always be together: never to part again.

Appreciation

I give thanks to God for my wonderful husband, Donnie, who has faithfully walked with me down this road of healing. Thank you, Donnie, for your love and for being my best friend.

I thank God for my son, Chezz, who encourages me in his own quiet way. I love you Chezz very much. Thank you.

To the greatest pastors Kenneth and Joyce Blease, thank you for your constant prayers and guidance. Thank you for your support. I love you both.

Thank you "Vickie" for your help and patience with me. Thank you for your friendship, and for seeing the vision of this book along with me.

Introduction

Proverbs 18:21 says: "Life and Death are in the power of the tongue and they that love it shall eat the fruit there of." Sometime we say things we really don't mean, but the word spoken can never be recalled. That is why it is so important that we think before we speak. The word of God tells us that we can choose to speak "Life" or "Death". As you will see from my story I had people who loved me very much, but their words weren't chosen carefully. I didn't know what to do when words hurt. But I had a special place for that hurt.

It is so important that we speak words of life to our children and to other people around us. I'm so glad that the Holy Spirit is revealing the word of truth to his people. I 'm so glad that there have been obedient men and women of God who have stood up in the last twenty-five years and taught the truth. I hope by reading this book that you will see clearly how we can hurt one another with our words. Proverbs 16:24, "Pleasant words are as a honeycomb, sweet to the soul, and health to all the bones." Amazing to me that we can speak words of life to other people or we can speak words that make their heart sick. Negative words spoken to you can also make you physically sick. I believe we need to speak God's word over everyone and everything that we possess, blessings and not curses. I believe the word of God will change everything around you. The word of God is spirit and they are life. Proverbs 15:23, "A man has joy by the answer of his mouth: and a word spoken in due season how good it is!" I want to be the person that will speak a word in due season to the people around me. Job 19:2, "how long will you vex my soul with your words." Vex in the Greek translation means to grieve or to cause pain. Job was saying to his friend how long are you going to cause me sorrow with your words. Even back in Job days, he knew the power of the tongue.

Father, I pray today that the words that proceed from my lips will be words of life to others. I pray that your words will control my tongue always and that I would always build and never destroy with my words.

My Life Begins

"You are a Bastard." A Bastard! I thought, what is a bastard? So one day when I was old enough to look up the word "bastard" in the dictionary, I learned that word meant, "one born out of wedlock, not genuine".

It was June 14, 1952, when I arrived into the world. I was born into a very large family. My mom, an unwed mother, lived with her parents. She had four brothers and four sisters. My mother was the oldest child. My grandparents loved me as if I was their own. It was fun growing up with such a large family. My mother fell in love with a widowed preacher and they were married when I was seven months old. My grandfather had grown attached to me and there was no way he was going to let "his bundle of joy" move out with my mother. My grandparents took me under their wings and raised me. They taught me the way of the Lord. There was no Sunday morning sleep-ins at my grandfather's home. The first thing we heard on Sunday morning was "Get yourself out of that bed and get ready to go to church! I can still hear his voice as he yelled only once to get us up, and we knew to "rise and shine". My grandparents are deceased now, and still today I am grateful for their love and care of me. My aunts and uncles all treated me like I was their baby sister.

When my mother married and moved out of the home of her parents, my Aunt Lois, the oldest of my mom's sisters, became my caretaker. I was seven months old and grew to love her as a mother. Oh, how I loved her. To me, she was my mother. She gave me my baths; she fed and slept with me. I loved her so very much! Then the day came when my little ears heard the unthinkable. My Aunt Lois was going away. Fear and rejection gripped my little heart. I didn't understand the feelings that I was experiencing, but I did know that I didn't like feeling that way.

I could hear everyone talking about how far she was going and how long it would be before my Aunt Lois would come back again. I was only two years old. I couldn't understand why she would want to leave me. I couldn't begin to think of a day without her presence. She had been there for me since the beginning for me. I knew no one else to love or to hold me as a mother holds a child. Yes, my grandparents loved me, but my aunt Lois had become my mother.

One particular morning I recall getting out of bed and rubbing my eyes remembering that this was the day that would change my life forever. I could hear voices of the family talking about my Aunt Lois leaving. Today was the day, and my heart pounded faster and faster each time I would hear someone say something about her leaving. Even now, forty-three years later, I can still feel the pain of that day. Why would she leave me, I thought in my heart. I could not understand. As the morning hours passed, I watched her as she began to pack her clothes. I was walking behind her every step crying, crying and begging her not to leave me. It was if my whole insides were shouting to her, "Don't leave me, please don't leave me". But she couldn't hear me. Why can't you hear me? Please don't leave me, while pulling on her clothes and hitting her on her legs. I stood in front of the dresser to stop her from getting her clothes, but nothing I did could stop her. I could see the excitement on her face; she was happy to leave the hard work on the farm and go to the big city. But she didn't know what I was feeling and didn't act as if she cared. I was just a little girl crying to my aunt Lois, but for me, this day would mark the beginning, that fear and rejection became my bosom buddies.

Loading her few belongings into the car, my every cry was "Don't leave me, don't go!" As I watched her go down the little dirt road that led to the farmhouse, again I felt the fear, rejection, and pain and the monster feeling of being unwanted. Even though, I didn't fully understand these feelings, I knew they were feelings I didn't like or know how to get rid of them.

Hours without my Aunt Lois turned into days. I would stand on the broken front porch and look down the little dirt road thinking how it would be if I could only see her coming back down the road, returning back home to me again. Days turned into months. It was a year before I would see her face again, only to go through the heartbreak of her leaving me again.

As time went by, I grew and time helped to ease the pain, but it never really went away. I just learned as a little girl to bury things that hurt. I found that it was easier to carry hurt and pain down into my little soul chest and pretend that they didn't exist.

Young brides have a "hope chest", a chest they can put things that they hope to use when they get married. In my case, I had a "soul chest", a place where I made deposits of all my hurts and pain.

Psalm 139: 13-18

Our Lord tells us in Psalms 139: verse 13, "for thou hast possessed my reins; thou hast covered me in my mother's womb. Thou hast possessed my reins" The word (reins) in the Hebrew translations means " the mind" (interior self) (the inner man). Praise be to God! Even in my mother's womb God knew that I would face the demon of fear and rejection. He had my emotions in his hand, though it would be many years before I would be rid of these oppressing spirits, God has been the keeper of my soul. Even from my mother womb there has been a plan and purpose for my life.

Thou has covered me in my mother's womb: verse 13; the word covered here in the Greek translation means (to fence in). In the beginning of my being God fenced me in and protected me. He is a good God, and he knew at my beginning what my days would hold. Verse 14. "I will praise you for I am fearfully and wonderfully made; marvelous are your works and that my soul knoweth right well. Yes my praise shall forever be to the God that created me.

I can say to you today that my soul, my mind, my emotions, knoweth full well that he is a God that will take care of you. Even when we are unaware, He is a God that will never leave you or forsake you. He is faithful.

Verse 17. How precious also are your thoughts unto me. Oh God! How great are the number of them. Verse 18. If I should count them, they are more in number than the sand of the sea. Awesome! What a thought. Just think about this scripture for a moment. His thoughts of us are more than the sand in the sea. That thought alone boggles my mind. To think his mind is always on me, and yes on you; with God there is no respect of person. He watches over us as precious jewels. There is not a second that God is not thinking about you and me. Imagine all the oceans and seas in the world. Now think about all the grains of sand there are in them. His word tells us that he thinks about us more than all the tiny pieces of sand. He said," My thoughts toward you are (more) than the sand of the sea". He is always thinking about you and me. I enjoy going to the beach in the summer.

I can look out across the vast amount of water and smile knowing that my father created it. Then, when I reach down and pick up a hand full of sand, taking my fingers rubbing through the tiny pieces, I have to shake my head in wonder. Knowing that he thinks about me more than all the sands in the seas. God loves you and me so very much. In fact, he loves us so much he gave his son (Jesus) that we might be his. John 3:16. For God so loved the world, (You and me), that he gave his only begotten Son that whosoever believeth in him should not perish, but have everlasting life.

Words That Hurt

When I was two years old and learning to walk, waking up early in the morning, sliding out of bed, thinking that my feet would never touch the floor. My husband Donnie, tells me there is no way I can remember that far back, but I can. I would finally make it to the bottom and the first thing that I would look for, before food, before play time, before anything, I would look for my grandmother's big Bible. My grandmother would take me in her lap and there in the kitchen door, in the sunlight, she would read me a Bible story and tell me about Jesus dying on the cross for me.

I had a Godly grandmother; she led her family in the ways of God, always praying for her children. At bedtime my grandparents would gather everyone in the living room and they would lead us in a family prayer. They were always thanking God for something.

My grandmother had this big flower garden with beautiful flowers. I would go inside the flower garden and pretend to play house. One day while playing in my favorite place, I heard my grandmother telling her friend that I did not know my daddy. I can remember thinking why don't I know my daddy? What about my grandpa, isn't he my daddy? The wheels in my head started turning. I wondered why I didn't know my daddy.

My grandmother's friend continued to stare at me as if she had lost something, but now, looking back, I know she was trying hard to figure out whom I resembled. I did what every little boy or girl would do, I began to ask questions. Who is my daddy? I couldn't understand why I didn't know my dad. I asked my grandmother and she looked at me as if to say, "What will I tell her?" She said, "Honey you don't have a daddy, your grandpa is your daddy". Now, nothing was making sense to me. Not knowing or being taught the power of the "tongue" and the "power of our words", my grandmother would usually say what came to her mind.

I couldn't understand what she was saying. The only point that I understood was that I didn't have a daddy. I would put these words of hurt in my secret hiding place, deep, deep down in my soul chest.

As I look back on my life at that age, I can't begin to explain how I learned at such an early age to bury the things that hurt me. I can only say that I believe every one that is brought into this world can, if they choose to, store up hurt and pain of any kind in the hiding place of the soul. Things that are too painful, things that we refuse to deal with, or if we are born again, things that we just never give to our father God and ask him to heal. Most of the time, we just pretend that it did not hurt, or we carry it deep down into our soul and we leave it there, ignoring that it is there.

My aunts and uncles, who all were teenagers, they all thought that I was their little baby. That put me in the position of listening to everyone and doing what everyone asked me to do. That was a difficult place for me. They all treated me as if they were my parents. It was hard for me to get away with anything.

Not only did I ask my grandmother about my Father, I

asked all of my aunts and uncles and they had no mercy on me. They just rattled off the first thing that came to their minds. The answers I got from them were, "You don't have a daddy. You were hatched," or the "buzzard's brought you here". Now, I know that might sound a little funny, but to a child three year old, it was heartbreaking. I just couldn't understand how other children had a father, but I did not. I was left confused that the love I felt for my grandpa could never be complete. Even though in my heart I felt that I loved him so very much, it could never be a "whole" love. Something was missing, "my real daddy". My mother married when I was seven months old, and I lived with my grandparents. My mother and husband had four children, three girls and a one boy. I loved my brother and sisters. As we all grew older, they found out that their father was not my real father. They began to call me their half-sister. I felt incomplete, as a child the word half-sister became part of their vocabulary. I would think, "Half is not whole".

As I grew older, I would hear the words "You don't belong here. You were a mistake", or "You don't have a daddy. "I was probably no more than seven years old at that time. I knew those words had to go in my little soul chest. I couldn't bear that thought. You might be thinking that I had awful aunts and uncles or that I was mistreated when I was a little girl. No, I wasn't. In fact, I was very much loved. My grandparents loved me with all their hearts. My aunts and uncles loved me also. They took care of me and watched over me just like any brother or sister would look after their younger sibling. But they did not know the power of the words that they were speaking. When they would call me a "bastard", those words were not spoken out of hate. It was spoken like today when sisters and brothers say little smart things to one another, but don't really mean any harm. I was the baby of that family and knew it and took advantage of all of the attention that I received.

Prisoner of the Soul

Proverbs 18:21 says, "Life and Death are in the power of the tongue." This is one of the greatest nuggets of wealth that I have ever received in the word of God. My life was totally turned around when God revealed this to me. We can speak life to ourselves, or we can speak death. In this same sense, we can speak words of death to those around us. The people whom we love so very much can be cursed by our words. By this truth in the word of God, you can see how the words that were spoken to me along with the, "fear and rejection" caused me to be a prisoner in my own soul. Psalm 142:7, "Bring my soul out of Prison, that I may praise you."

For many years the spirit of fear and rejection owned me as their salve. I was inferior and timid. I felt like I could never measure up to the standard of others. I always sought the approval of others. I wanted everyone to like me, and if they gave me the slightest reason that they didn't, it would tear me apart. Rejection was a cruel taskmaster.

Very little is said about our souls in the church. We hear so much about the spirit of man and the "Do's and Don'ts" of the flesh, but not many preachers or teachers teach on the soul. We really need to be taught on the soul of man. If you were to ask the majority of the church the question, what is the soul of man? They would not know what to answer.

Psalms 23:3, "He restoreth my soul; he leadeth me in the path of righteousness for his name's sake".

Question? If our Lord restores our soul, don't you think, that we need to be able to identify what our soul consists of? King David said: "Unto you, O Lord, do I lift up my soul".

Every person has a soul. The soul of man consists of our mind, will and emotions. This is where I had my little hidden chest in the pit of my soul. No one could enter and no one knew where my hiding place was located. I believe that there are those of you who are reading this book and realizing, that you also have that hiding place that you visit from time to time, storing up hurt and pain that you don't know what to do with. Maybe the pain is too great to deal with, or maybe you just keep ignoring it hoping that one day it will disappear. Would you like for me to tell you the truth? It will never disappear. If you have suffered any kind of hurt and pain of the soul it will always be there. And each time you face any kind of situation that resembles the hurt you harbor, your soul will open up and that hurt will reveal itself. I believe the first place that hurt reveals itself is in our mind. Our thought life is connected to our soul. The hurt in our soul will send a signal to our thoughts and say, "Warning! Warning! You've been hurt like that before". And instantly you will remember the person or incident that caused you that hurt.

I pray for you that, after reading this book you will be willing to let our Lord deliver your soul. Jesus is our deliverer!

I was raised on a farm in North Carolina. My grandpa worked very hard to keep the family going and to supply food for all the children in the house. In the time of planting, there were times of revival at the little country church we attended. They schedule a weeklong revival, having service twice a day. My grandpa and grandma would come out of the field at 1:00 p.m. and be at church by 2:00 p.m. for the afternoon service. The power of the Holy Spirit would fall on the faithful few that would make the sacrifice to be there for the afternoon service. Then they would return to the field and continue working until evening. Once again, they would go back to the church at 7:00 p.m. for the night service. Now, I would call that a sacrifice. God has always been a part of my life. I was taught that there was a God and I had the fear of God in me, but I must say I wasn't taught the full knowledge of the word God. I was taught, as much as they knew to teach me. We had the "Hell Fire and Brimstone preachers". They put more fear than knowledge in us.

Starting school was a day of joy for me. I was looking forward to going the "big" school as I called it for a long time. The first day of school was really difficult for me. I had all those negative thoughts inside my head telling me that I could not do what the other children were doing. I was two weeks late starting school, because I had gotten sick just before the school season began. The class routine had already begun. When I saw what the other boys and girls were doing, I was terrified. All I could hear in my mind was "you cannot do it," and I was paralyzed. Finally, one day the teacher called on me to read from the Dick and Jane book. I couldn't speak a word. I could only hear, "What if I'm wrong?" I went through grammar school thinking that I could not do the work. I did not make good grades. I just got by. So many times I was asked to go up to the chalkboard and write a sentence or do a math problem only to be laughed at by the other children. I made a lot of deposits in my hiding place of my soul. I went through school feeling timid and afraid most of the time.

Life and Death

One night around 7:00 p.m., I was lying on the sofa in the living room, and I was not feeling well. My grandma had taken me to the doctor that day. I had a high fever and a stomachache. The cause was unknown. I had an excuse to stay out of school. It was special for me. When I was sick, I could ask for anything and my grandpa would do it. Anything I wanted, my grandpa would say. "Just name it baby girl." I would ask for Donald Duck orange juice in the can. I can still see my grandpa in his overalls, putting on his old worn coat, then out the front door, just for me. I would listen intently to hear his old truck crank up and down the road he would go, to get my heart's desire. Just as I listened to hear him leave, I would listen to hear his return. Joy would fill my heart. This was a treat for me. It was seldom that I received anything from the country store. Getting sick was kind of a treat for me.

That evening there was a gentle knock at the front door. "Come in" I heard my grandpa say. The door slowly opened and in walked this stranger, tall and well dressed. "Hello" he said to my grandparents. My grandparents were surprised. "Well, well" said my grandpa, "I haven't seen you in years".

They reacquainted themselves and talked about the time that had gone by. My grandma, glancing at me with a little smile finally spoke up and said, "John, do you know who this is?" Looking over at me lying on the sofa, he turned and stared at me. He responded, "No I don't believe I know this pretty little girl." Well, my grandmother proceeded to tell him I was his brother Henry's little girl. She said, "You remember when Henry was coming over here to see Mary? This is his little girl. Her name is Faye." A silence came over the room. I knew that something was wrong. I could tell the announcement my grandma just made, was not a joyful one. "Well, is that right?" said John, looking at me in amazement. I could tell the stop he made to say "Hello" to an old acquaintance was a big mistake for him. This visit must end now. So he put on his nice long coat and hat, said his goodbye as if to say, "I'm sorry I stopped by". The front door slowly closed. My grandparents, not knowing the power of the spoken word began to talk to one another. They talked long and hard about the situation of my birth. My grandma said, "Well, whether he wants to admit it or not this is Henry's child. She looks just like his sister. He knew when she was born, because Fred, made sure he knew". "Well," said my grandpa as he was coming over to sofa to put his hand on my forehead to check for fever, "I love this little gal." I knew my grandparents loved me, but what I had just experienced was a major blow. I didn't understand the whole picture of what just had taken place. But one thing I did know, the look on this stranger's face would go with me the rest of my life. The words spoken by my grandparents after the stranger left explained the look in his eyes. Again, I was not wanted. Lying on the sofa I took a little trip down the stairs of my heart, down to deepest part of my soul; and there I made a major deposit in my secret hiding place. It seemed as I grew older, the deposit became larger and more hurtful.

Satan's Strongholds

When a child goes through life receiving nothing but rejection and criticism, the accuser of the brethren, "Satan" is able to maintain a huge stronghold in his life. The spirits of accusation, criticism, judgment, rejection and fear follow children throughout their lives. It always seems as if people are constantly coming against that child or person with their tongue. In many cases, the root of rejection has to be cut, before the enemy's stronghold of negative words spoken over that person can be broken. More often than not, a child is held back from success in life because of words spoken over them in the past. This stronghold can be pulled down and the assignment of Satan can be canceled.

Isaiah 54:17, says

"No weapon that is formed against you shall prosper; and every tongue (word) that shall rise against you in judgment, you shall condemn. This is your inheritance as a servant of the Lord and your righteousness is of him saith the Lord." When you know the Lord Jesus Christ as Lord and Savior, there is hope. No longer do you have to stay under the curse of rejection. When the enemy comes against you with condemnation through words or thoughts he gives you, you can remember that you have the victory, in the name of Jesus. You can declare that your righteousness is of him. Then the enemy has no foothold to continue his wounding of you with his words of rejection. You destroy his stronghold. Praise be to God!

My Cinderella Story

At the age of fifteen, my grandma opened her own little country store. I was the one who was left in charge while my grandma did other things that needed to be done. There was no one there but me. Looking out the window of the little store, I saw this young guy whom I had never seen before get out of the truck and start pumping gas. Like any fifteen- year- old girl, I made sure my hair was in place. He finished pumping the gas and came inside to pay. We looked at one another and there was an immediate attraction. There were not too many words spoken, just "Hello," and "Thank-you," but I knew that he would be back to buy more gas. He came back that same day. I wasn't in the store, but through my bedroom window I saw him. I walked out on the front porch to let him know that I was there. I didn't want him to know that I was excited to see him stopping again. I guess you could say that I was playing it "cool".

The next day I wanted to keep the store for my grandma, she didn't have to ask. I went on my own. About eleven o'clock a.m. the blue and white truck drove up again. Back for more gas so soon. I didn't think so. I knew there had to be an interest there. Again, he walked in to pay for his gas, and a conversation began. He asked me about myself, and I asked about him. He asked me if I would go to the movies with him, and of course I said yes. I answered yes, as if I went out on a date every weekend. My grandparents kept the "rope pretty tight" on me when it came to the opposite sex. All I could do was pray that my grandpa would be in a good mood when I asked him if I could go to the movies with this young man. I didn't know how my grandpa was going to handle that. I had only been out with one boy, and my grandpa always gave me a certain time to be in. The date could not last more than two hours. This young man had asked me out to see a movie. I would somehow have to talk my grandpa into this.

His name was Kenny and he told me about his family. His father was a minister. I thought this might be a plus for my grandpa. My next task would be to somehow get my grandpa's permission.

I walked over to my grandparents, who were resting on the porch from a hard day's work, and began to tell them about Kenny. As I told them about him and his family, I saw in my grandpa's eye a twinkle of approval. "Oh yeah!" My grandpa said. "I know his father. He is a wealthy man. His name is Ken Canady. He's well thought of all over the county. Wow! I thought what is this and who is this that has asked me out for a date. I felt like Cinderella. Grandpa talked about their family and told us all he knew about them. Finally, I felt like I had gained enough ground to ask the big question. "Mama, I asked, do you think that I could go to the movies with Kenny on Friday night?" "I knew that if I asked my grandma in front of my grandpa, I would have a better chance of getting permission from him. After all, how could they say no after all the good things they had said about his father? My grandpa looked at my grandma. He would always take his beloved time when I asked him a question that I really didn't want to ask. Finally, he opened his mouth and said", "You can go, but…. (There was always a but.) "You must be back at 9:00 p.m". I knew that would be a problem, so I explained to him that the movie wouldn't be over until around 10:00 p.m. Surprisingly enough, he agreed. That was the happiest day of my life. I walked on "cloud nine" for three days, just waiting for Friday night to come. The thought of someone asking me out on a date with his background and knowing that his dad was well to do was really overwhelming for me. Boys from a different back ground never looked at me twice. Frankly, I think that was my first movie. Back in those days the rich were friends with the rich, and the poor knew their place, with the poor. This was really the story of Cinderella. Kenny called me on the telephone, and I told him the date was on, and of course there was more gas for the truck. Friday night finally rolled around. It seemed like a month since I had asked my grandpa for permission to go out, but it had only been three days. I was oh so anxious all that day. Kenny pulled up in the driveway right on time and my heart was beating fast. A knock on the door and a "come in", by my grandpa started a dream come true for me. That evening wasn't like any I had ever experienced. There was a special feeling between us both, and I knew it would last, and he felt the same. After the second date, third date, fourth date, he finally said the words I wanted to hear. He said he was falling in love with me those were the words I longed to hear. I told him that I felt the same, and a wonderful romance began. My family seemed to be happy for me. Kenny won the friendship of my family and friends. I met his family and was accepted as one of their own. I had a good relationship with Kenny's family. Kenny had three sisters and two brothers and wonderful parents. His mother was a loving, caring woman and made me feel like I was always at home.

Kenny asked me to marry him, and I accepted. I was sixteen and Kenny was one week into his eighteenth birthday.

We were two kids taking the responsibility of adults. Six months after we were married, his father (who was a contractor), built us our first home. It was beautiful. It wasn't uncommon for a young girl and boy to be married at such an early age in those days, but it was uncommon for such a young couple to have a new home just starting out in a marriage. We were blessed. I guess you could say Cinderella had finally arrived; at least that was the way I felt. I had grown up not having a lot, but I had just entered into a whole new lifestyle; having everything my heart desired, and I liked that very much. I haven't mentioned the Lord, because he was nowhere in our decision to be married. The decision was made without the guidance of God. We eventually started going to church and gave our heart to the Lord. We had a good life and everything seemed to be going so well. When I was nineteen, I had my first child (a baby girl) She was so precious: 3lbs and 2ozs, a little bundle from Heaven. It was a difficult pregnancy, but with the help of God she survived. The doctor told us that our baby would have to weigh at least 5 lbs, before she could be released from the hospital. She had to stay eight weeks, but Kenny and I visited her every day, looking forward to the day we could take her home with us. The nursery was ready, and everyone in both families was excited. She was the first grandchild in Kenny's family and also in the family of my mother. December 24th the phone rang early that morning, and it was the doctor. He was calling to tell us that we could pick up our little precious one. What a Christmas present God was giving us. We were overwhelmed with joy. We dressed as quickly as we could, and for me there were no words to express the joy. We arrived at the hospital, and the nurses seemed to be as excited as we were. They knew how much we loved her and wanted her home. They had put her into this big Christmas stocking with a little Santa hat on her very tiny head. It was so precious. We finally walked out with our gift from the Lord. We were so happy. We gave her the name,

"Tonya Michelle". My grandpa said, "I'll never be able to pronounce her name correctly." But eventually he got the hang of it. She was the joy of everyone's heart. I was a young mother with a live, breathing, baby doll, and she was my reason for living.

Sixteen months later, I was pregnant with my second child. This pregnancy went well and again the joy of another child filled the house. On August 23, 1972, I give birth to a healthy baby girl. She also was a gift from the Lord. We named her Tina LoRelle. I really had my hands full, but I loved every moment of it. The children were my heart.

August 31,1976 God blessed Kenny and me with another beautiful little girl. We named her "Tara La'chelle". She was the baby that would take our hearts. She had her own little way of winning everyone's heart. All the hurt and pain of the past seemed to be a faded dream. The hidden chest of my soul was nowhere to be found. I was living a dream come true. Everything that a young couple could ask for: three precious baby girls, a new home and a car. If there was ever a need, we had Kenny's parents. They were always there to help us, and to meet our every need.

I had everything that a young woman could ask for. The only thing that we didn't have was a true relationship with God. We went to church and did all the good deeds, but knowing God, we didn't. When I said early that we gave our hearts to the Lord, we only went through the ritual. To be really honest with you, I don't think Kenny and I really ever saw the need to be totally connected to God. We had everything here on this earth anyone could ask for, but we were about to find out that a house built without the Lord would be a house that would not stand.

A House Divided
Will Not Stand

Kenny and I were married for eleven years. In eleven years we separated fourteen times. The first three years of our marriage was wonderful. But the home that we built without the Lord, was a home that crumbled into ashes. I found myself-standing in the ashes of a marriage with three little girls. They were so innocent. They didn't deserve to be in such a place of misery. Kenny and I both were unhappy. We tried to work our marriage out for the sake of the girls, but to no avail. Each time that we tried, the circumstances of our marriage got worse. And to repeat a terrible situation would only bring hurt and pain to the ones involved. Matthew 12:25, Jesus said: "Every kingdom divided against itself is brought to desolation: and every house divided against itself shall not stand." This scripture is so true. Kenny and I were certainly divided. I finally I realized that our marriage was beyond repair. The damage was too great for the both of us. Once the trust is broken in a marriage, only the grace of God can restore. If trust is not in a marriage, you have no peace. And peace is the bond of love. Instead of peace Kenny and I had strife and contention constantly. It was not a good situation.

I decided for my girl's sake, that it would be better for them to live with their father. With him, they wouldn't have to leave their home again. Separating fourteen times within eleven years was too much moving and rearranging of our life. Each time Kenny and I separated, the girls and I would go back to my grandparent's home. This happened too often; it should never have happened the first time. I made up my mind, that this would be best for my girls.

Decision!

I awaken on Monday morning with my heart beating fast, when I realized that today will be the day I would leave. It was hard for me to believe that my life had come to this. I would give Kenny custody of the girls, and I had the visiting rights. There wasn't another way. This was the only solution I could see. Having my mind made up, I left while they slept. That would be the easiest way for them. It certainly wasn't easy for me. I knew in my heart that I could never say goodbye to my little girls.

I put all my things in my car, and tiptoed into their bedrooms and quietly looked at my girls. I said goodbye in my heart, and I turned and walked out of their room and out the door. I got in my car, drove out of the driveway onto the road and just stared into space. I couldn't believe that I had left my girls. I told myself to keep going, and not to look back. I had to do this. This I thought was the right thing to do. (Over and over, I repeated those words to myself. My foot on the gas pedal, and saying to myself, you have gone this far, you must keep on going.) My thoughts were, I must live a separate life from my babies, my precious little girls. This was best for them. The further I went, the more I was convinced that it was final. I knew there was no turning back. I could imagine the talk in town, about how Mr. Canady's daughter-in-law left her three children, but only I knew the truth. I continued to tell myself, that I could not turn back, no matter what anyone said or thought. I would do what I thought best for my children.

As I entered Charlotte, North Carolina I was so confused and dazed from the stress of leaving, the two-hour drive turned into what seemed to be days and days of driving. Scared and alone for the first time in my life, I sat there in a parking lot thinking about my children. I knew that the past two hours had changed my life forever. Little did I know just how much my life would change?

I got out of the car, walked over to the phone booth to call my Aunt Betty. When Aunt Betty answered I said, "This is Faye". The tears and pain of what I had just done two hours before came out of me full blast. Please I said, "Come and get me. I have left. I have left". She told me to stay right where I was, and she would be there in five minutes. I got back in my car with the thought that I could not believe that I had actually left my girls. As hard as it was and as much as my heart hurt, as I weighed it in the balance, I felt that I had done what was right. Aunt Betty pulled up beside me and told me to follow her. I followed her back to her home and was welcomed with open arms. My Aunt Betty knew about the situation, so there wasn't a need to do much explaining to her and Uncle Charlie. They comforted me as much as anyone could.

I explained to them what I had decided to do about my children. I told them I wanted to get a job, and maybe one day the girls could come live with me whenever I got on my feet. I knew deep in my heart that I could never make it on my own with three children. I had tried so many times before and failed. This was only a hope, a dream, and a longing desire. I asked my Aunt Betty to please not tell anyone where I was. I wanted to do that in my own time. She agreed, long as I was comfortable with my decision.

I thought the first night away from my babies was the worst night of my life. I missed them so much. I sat with Aunt Betty and her family and watched television. Everyone was focused on me, trying to help me to feel better. I had spent the day crying, trying to come to terms with my decision. Lying in the guest bedroom with the window open, I could hear the frogs and the sound of a train that came by every night exactly at 11:00 p.m. It was a very lonely sound, and I was feeling the way the train sounded. "God" I would say, "I love my little girls!" I was sure that God was the last one who wanted to hear my voice. I could hear the voices of my relatives. I could imagine what my grandmother was saying. I could just imagine what the whole county was saying, and I knew that it was not "a good report". Then my mind would take me to the bedside of my little girls. I could see my girls with my mind's eye. Lord, I would say, I can't believe that I have left my babies. The realization of what I had done was becoming more and more real and very heavy on my heart.

Three days went by and I was a big mess! I couldn't stop crying. I tried to join in with the family activities. They tried so hard to make me feel better. As each day went by there was a knot in my chest that just got bigger and bigger with every passing minute. "God", I would sigh, I want to see my girls," but I knew in my heart that my decision was a final one.

On the fourth day away from my girls I couldn't stand it any longer, I had to hear their voices. Aunt Betty had been asking me to call and let my grandmother know where I was. I agreed to take that big step to call my grandmother and let her know that I was fine. I would try explaining my decision to her.

I was too afraid to call my grandmother so I decided to

call Susan my younger sister. I could call her and find out the latest news in town. She began to tell me what everyone was saying. It was just as I had imagined. I was now known as the woman who left her three children to pursue a life of bright lights and parties. At the end of the conversation, I could hardly breathe. My chest was so tight. I made arrangements with my sister to pick up the girls and bring them to my grandmother's house so I could talk to them. I put the phone down and went to the kitchen door. Aunt Betty followed me. The tears were falling, and my heart was aching. I explained to her what the people at home were saying. She comforted me, and told me that she knew it must hurt to hear what all the people were saying about me. She reassured me that I knew the reason I left. I did know, but it still didn't make the hurt go away. Not only was I feeling the hurt and loneliness of my girls but now everyone's opinion. The word was; that I walked out on my three children and left them behind for the party lifestyle.

I could hardly wait until 11:00 a.m. When I would get to talk to my babies. When the phone rang, it was my sister Sue. She told me the girls were there. "Let me talk to them," I said. I was so excited! "Hello", I heard on the other end. "Hello Baby", I said. My oldest daughter asked me where I was and when was I coming home. I told her that it would not be long. I told her that I would go to pick them up and go to grandma's house for the weekend. My daughter replied, "O.K. mama, I'm going to play with Tammy now." The phone was passed to the middle daughter, Tina, "Hey, mama," she said. I said, " Hey, my little girl." Tina said, "I miss you, I love you, and when are you coming home?" I told her the same thing that I had told my oldest daughter, Tonya. Next was my precious baby, Tara, the youngest. She just wanted me to come home. I tried with everything in me to help her understand, but how do you explain to a two year old, why her mother is no longer with her! After talking to the girls, I asked my sister what kind of attitude Kenny had when she picked up the children. She said, "He was fine, and he said that he would not try to keep the girls from you".

After that first phone call, I realized that I had given up my rights to my babies and knew a door had closed in my life. I would never be able to enter through that door again. I would never be able to be a mother to the children that I had borne.

A few days later I decided that I needed to go to the doctor. I wasn't eating or sleeping and depression had taken root in my soul. I couldn't do anything but cry and long for my girls. I went to Aunt Betty's doctor. When the doctor came in he asked me what was going on. I told him that I couldn't eat and I needed some medication that would increase my appetite. I had lost 4lbs in five days. He asked me what was going on in my life and I finally had to tell him assuming that if I didn't he wasn't going to give me the medication I needed. I told him I had given my husband custody of my three girls and how terribly I missed them. I told him I thought it best for the girls to stay with their daddy, because he was financially able to take care of them. I looked up at the doctor as I was telling him my situation and there on his cheeks were tears. He told me how sorry he was to hear that. He said, "Sometimes we have to do what we think is best for our children." He said, he knew I felt guilty for the decision I had made, but he understood.

My little soul chest had tipped over and spilt all over the place. My life had turned upside down, but I would do the best that I could to survive.

I knew I had to get over these feelings of loneliness and missing my babies. The next morning I started job hunting. I found a job with a construction company. They called me the "gopher", I was the person designated to handle pick-ups and deliveries for the company's additional job sites.

After I learned my way around Charlotte, I enjoyed the job.

Kenny's girlfriend moved in with him and the girls. She had two girls about the same age as my two oldest girls. Now the girls had someone to look after them, and they seemed to be fine with the new addition. Of course, having other children to play with made it seem like lots of fun.

It was time to make the trip back home. I would have to face everyone and their criticism. I knew that I had made the right decision. I decided it was time to take a trip to my soul chest and put some stuff away so that it wouldn't hurt so much when I came face to face with my critics. This would be the first time that I'd seen anyone since the morning that changed my life forever. I would put all the words they had spoken about me and all the names they called me deep inside my secret place so that nothing could hurt me.

It was Friday evening and two weeks had passed. I was on my way home to get my girls. I drove into the driveway and the door opened. Out ran my precious little girls. They were so pretty. Each one had their little overnight bags dragging behind them. Oh, I was so happy to see them. Kenny came walking out behind them. Hugs and kisses were the order of the day. They were so happy to see me. It was hard to contain ourselves. Finally, off to grandmother's house we go. So far, the plan seemed to be working. The girls seemed to be adjusting to their new lifestyle, and I was somehow finding a life, I thought. I had a job, a place to live, and the girls had a home. My plan had worked.

Several months had passed and it seemed to me that everything was working out. The girls seemed happy and Kenny seemed to be doing a good job with them. The girls liked his girlfriend, and it appeared that she was taking very good care of them. As for me, I was still working and trying to adapt to the new lifestyle that I had chosen. It was very hard for me to sit and be quiet because all of the emotions that were surfacing I didn't have a clue as to how to handle them. All I knew was, I had made a big decision that had altered my life. I was going to have to stand up and accept the consequences of that decision.

Four months had gone by, and each time I returned home to be with my girls the names people had labeled me with, became worse and worse. Kenny made it clear to everyone that he had custody of the girls. The word around town was that I just packed up one day out of the blue and left. It was sad for me to know that I could not prove that this was not the case. When I went to town or to the grocery store with the girls or alone, the look I received from people was a look of disgust. After all, I had been labeled the "woman who packed up and left her children".

Those things bothered me greatly, but I knew that I could not prove differently. Because the way I left, it did look as if I left one day without a care. So, there was a lot of time that I would visit my little soul chest to make deposits of hurt and pain. Soon, it became a daily thing.

Several more months had gone by, and guilt and loneliness were more than I could stand. I missed my babies and; I missed home and my loved ones. I told myself that Charlotte was my new home. It was not far away, however, it was not close enough to the children I loved so much.

During one of the times that Kenny and I separated. I had met a man that I thought I could love and be happy with. I got in touch with him and explained what had taken place in my life. It wasn't long before he relocated to Charlotte. I was hoping that he could make a difference in my life. The truth is my life was turned upside down again. We moved in together, and by the end of January 1980, I knew I had walked out of one disappointing relationship into another. I couldn't tell anyone. I had nowhere to go and no one to turn to. Aunt Betty had warned me to be careful, but I didn't listen. I was at the end of my rope and my life was terrible. I just wanted to be happy and have peace, but with every passing day, I could see my life dissolving right before my eyes. I felt like I was climbing a slippery mountain.

One day I sat down and wrote grandma a letter. I told her that she must know how much I loved my girls and missed them. I told her I wanted my girls back. I asked my grandmother to pray for me that God would give me my babies back. My grandma told me she prayed for me every day. She told me how she prayed that God would save me. When I read that part, I thought, "I know, but right now what I really need is for God to give me my babies back".

The Knock at the Door!

It was Friday, February 8, 1979, and I was getting off work, excited about going home to be with the girls. I hadn't seen them in two weeks. I was picking up the girls every two weeks instead of every week, because of the strain on them and myself. Separating on Sunday evening was hard on everyone. I thought, that every two weeks might be better, and it would give them more time to adjust. It seemed to me that the longer we stayed apart, the worse it was for them and me. I hated the thought of putting them off at their dad's house. They would cry, and I would cry. I knew this was the only way. Maybe one day they would understand. And maybe one day my heart would stop hurting.

Driving into the parking lot at the apartment complex where Bill and I were living, I jumped out of the car and ran inside to start packing. I was ready for my weekend to get started. I knew it would take me at least two hours to get home. So by 7:00 p.m. I should be picking up the girls. As I was about ready to put my things in the car, Bill walked in and said he didn't think I should leave, because the weatherman was predicting lots of snow. It had already started snowing. I pulled the curtain back and looked outside. He was right. The snow was falling.

I knew that I could not drive in that type of weather, not by myself anyway. Even if Bill would offer to go with me, we would probably get stranded on the road. The snow was falling too hard to try to make that drive that night. I thought, maybe I can leave in the morning maybe it will stop soon. I decided that I would wait until morning putting my bags down with disappointment. I thought no one in their right mind would drive in those conditions. My 1967 Volkswagen was in no shape to make a trip home in the snow. It was a good little car, but not that good.

Bill and I went to the grocery store and came home and cooked. We enjoyed some movies and a couple of glasses of wine. By 11:00 p.m., the snow was really coming down. We both decided to go to bed. Lying there in the dark bedroom I could see the shadows of the tree branches moving back and forth, and I lay there gazing out into the dark night. I wondered about my girls. I knew Kenny would at least explain to them about the snow; how I was not able to drive down to pick them up. I was hoping he would explain that their mother would probably come the next day to pick them up. Those were my thoughts. I could hear Bill breathing deeply. He had already fallen asleep. Something else I remember that was rather strange to me. I had been awakened for the last two nights, by the dogs that lived across the street from us. We had been living there two months, and a lady had a dog kennel connected to her property. The past two nights, those dogs had awakened me with their terrible howling. I wondered if they would waken me again tonight.

I finally went to sleep with thoughts about hopefully going home the next morning. Around 2:30 a.m. I was awakened by a loud knock at the door. I heard my Uncle Jr. calling my name. I must be dreaming, I thought. Trying to wake up enough to make sense of what I heard, I thought it couldn't be my Uncle Jr., because my Aunt Betty was the only one who knew where I lived. Again, I heard him call my name. He said, "Faye", open the door!" By that time I was jumping out of the bed. Trying to feel my way around the bedroom, so I could get to the front door where I heard his voice calling me. From the bedroom to the living room, to the front door, I went stumbling around trying to wake up enough to make some kind of sense of what was going on. I reached the door and before I could unlock it, again there was a loud knock and a call for "Faye". I knew it was my Uncle Jr. Why was he here at 2:30 in the morning? Why was he calling out to me in such a voice of despair? How did he find me anyway? All these thoughts were rushing through my mind. As I was opening the door fast as I could, I heard a voice say to me. (I have them now and the only way you can get them is through me). I didn't understand what I had just heard; or who was saying this to me. All I knew was I needed to get the door unlocked, and find out what was going on!

Finally, I got the door unlocked. Bill was standing behind me when I opened the door. When I opened the door; there was my Uncle Jr., my two sisters, and my brother-in-law. I knew without a doubt, something terrible had happened. I cried out, "What's wrong?" What's wrong! My Uncle had put his arms around me, holding me. He said, "Honey, there has been a car wreck and they have been killed!" I was engulfed by grief, sorrow and loss. I had lost all sense of reason. All I knew was that one of my babies was dead. I didn't understand my uncle Jr. when he said all my babies were dead. Finally they got me dressed. I could hear my Uncle Jr. telling Bill that the car went into the river. My heart was dying. I didn't know which one of my babies had left me. I did know that I was dying with sorrow. They put me into the car and we started to back out of the driveway. I gained enough strength to ask my Uncle Jr. who was holding me, saying nothing. I asked which of my girls had died, not wanting to know, but I had to know. When I asked him, he said, "All of them baby, all of them!" At that time; that very second, my heart was crushed into a million pieces. I always used the example of my grandfather making sausage when I was a little girl. I used to watch him put a whole piece of meat in the sausage grinder and out the other end would come a million pieces. That is the way my heart felt. If I tried to tell you how I felt, I know I would fail. Words can't describe it.

Job 6:2,3, Job said, "Oh that my sadness and troubles were weighed. For they are heavier than the sand of a thousand seashores. I could look old brother Job in the eye and say to him, "Mr. Job been there, done that!" Surely the grief was more than I could bear.

Psalm 6:7, David said, "Mine eye is consumed with grief." This was true for me; I was dying with every breath I took.

It took forever to get to my grandma's house. All the way there I was praying that someone would please wake me up. This has to be a horrible nightmare. I would tell God under my breath, "Please Lord! Please let someone wake me up!" Entering inside the city limits of my hometown, there was a sense of Holy hush, because of the terrible thing that had happened earlier, right outside the city limits of that little town on that cold snowy afternoon.

Before they took me to my grandmother's house, my Uncle Jr. insisted that I go to the hospital and let the doctor give me something to calm me, but there was no medication a doctor could give me that could help or reach where I was. As the doctor gave me the shot, he repeated over and over, "I'm sorry. I'm so sorry". It had been about three hours since I had heard the unthinkable about my children. Turning onto the rocky paved road that led up to my grandmother's house I could see car lights on both sides of the road. As far as I could see, there were car lights. It seemed as if there were hundreds of cars on that road that led to grandma's house. If there had been any doubt in my mind that maybe I really was asleep, there wasn't any then. My God, I thought. It is true! It's true! Oh God, my babies are gone!

Driving down the driveway to the house where I was raised, I saw so many friends, family, people I knew, and even people I didn't know. It was 4:30 a.m. and the road, yard, and house were filled with people. Everyone was silent as the door opened and they carried me inside the house. Going into the house, I looked up and saw my grandmother's face first. All I could say was, "My babies, my babies, my babies!" They put me on the bed in my grandma's bedroom. There I could look out the window, and I could see, as the morning sun peeked through the trees, my little girls running through the yard playing like I'd seen them do so many times before.

I was a dead woman! I knew that I could never live nor did I want to. I couldn't see my life without my girls, and I didn't want my life without them. The pain and the sorrow were too great for me. People were coming and going, hundreds, one after the other, but I couldn't see them. I couldn't hear them. The place where I was, no one could reach me. The next day people were still coming and going to give me their regrets, but still no one could help me. Lying on the bed I could hear the people talking as they went in and out. I could hear the conversations in the kitchen. I could hear one say "You can be sure that God will only take so much before his mercy runs out." I could hear another say, " You will reap just what you sow." Still another saying, "If only she hadn't left her children, they would be alive today, instead of laying in a funeral home."

God I can't stand this! I can't stand this pain! I can't stand this guilt! I can't stand this sorrow! God, I can't stand the thought of being without my girls! I don't want to live,

God! Why did you take my babies, Lord? God, you know I loved my babies! They were all I had Lord! Why? I did everything I knew to do, Lord. Why did they have to leave me?

Laying and staring into the ceiling, one tear after another fell down my cheeks. If only it had just been one of them Lord, even two, but God, you took them all at one time. These were my thoughts. I didn't do much talking. Maybe a yes or no was about as much as I could utter.

Twenty-four hours had passed since I received the terrible news about my girls. My aunt came into the bedroom where I was, and I finally got the words out. Please tell me what happened? She said Kenny's girlfriend had taken my girls along with her two girls to get ice cream, and on the way back the rain turned into snow and made the roads slippery. She lost control of the car on the curve at the river. The car slid into the river. Heather managed to get out with her youngest daughter, but Tonya, Tina, Tara and Heather's oldest daughter did not make it out. Oh no, I didn't know, she lost a child too. There were four little girls who went home to be with God that night. I felt this was the result of my decision I made on that September morning. I was the blame. I was devastated.

Two days later, still unable to do anything except go to the bathroom (and I had help doing that), I could still hear whispers. I knew that my family was trying to keep something from me. My aunt Clara came in where I was laying and said, "Faye we need to tell you something. They haven't found Tonya yet." How much more can I bear Lord? No doubt, I will die, I thought to myself. I thought about Hell and thought about trying to live a life without my girls and Hell looked much easier. As a fresh stream of tears flowed from my eyes, I told myself it wouldn't be long, and I wouldn't be feeling this pain. I couldn't bear this thing that had happened to me. God, please help me, I cried.

Time to Say Goodbye

It was time to go to the funeral home for the wake, and I didn't want to go. Driving to the funeral home, again with my Uncle Jr. holding me, there was no strength in me. Uncle Jr. walked with me every step, and for that I thanked him. As I was walking into the funeral home, again there was that Holy hush. I walked down the hallway to go into the room where my babies laid. As I turned to go in, I was praying to God. I didn't want to see them like this. I lifted my head as I entered the room. I looked and my eyes saw for the first time what my ears had heard, and my heart had felt. My precious little girls lying lifeless. All I could see and hear was the last time I was with them. "Mommy, we don't want you to live in Charlotte. We want you to stay with us". It was so hard to leave them that last Sunday, but I felt in my heart that I had chosen the best for them.

I had no hope for life. All I desired was to die with them. The next day, Sunday, was the day we would lay my two little girls to rest. They had not found the body of my oldest daughter, Tonya. They had been searching around the clock, but to no avail. The tragedy was such a loss for me that I didn't have enough tears for all the sorrow and grief. The funeral was at Kenny's home church. Kenny did come to my grandparent's home during that time, but I vaguely remember the visit. I had no contact with Kenny, so I didn't know what to expect. There was no resistance in me, and I really didn't care at that moment. All I knew was that as soon as I was alone, I was going to make my exit. If there was a Hell, then so be it. The funeral, I can't remember much about. I was drowning in my tears. I remember the three small coffins, and I remember that on Tonya's coffin, they had her picture, because they had not found a body. Also, from the house to the church and from the church to the gravesite, there was not a "hello" between Kenny and me or a "goodbye". There was only silence between us.

Sunday evening, after the funeral, I laid in my grandmother's bed counting down the hours that I would finally be by myself. Then I would be able to get the sleeping pills that the doctor had prescribed to help me sleep. There had been no sleep for me. I had not slept since Friday night. I fell asleep wondering if Kenny explained to the girls that I could not drive in the snow, and that I could go the next morning. Little did I realize that my little angels were already with the Lord!

The accident happened around 5:30 p.m. and that was about the time that I was looking at the snow through the window deciding whether it would be best for me to wait until morning. I had no one who could comfort my aching heart. So many tried, but no one could help.

Lamentations 1:2, "She weepeth sore in the night, and her tears are on her cheeks: Among all her lovers she hath none to comfort her: all her friends have dealt treacherously with her, they have become her enemies."

This describes the way that I was feeling at that time. My heart was dying. My cheeks had not been dry since that Friday around 2:30 a.m. when the knock came at the door. I had heard all the words that had been spoken against me.

The words "You must pick yourself up and try to keep going", "You can't undo what has already been done," "No good in crying now, you should have thought about this before you left them" and "If she just hadn't left them." I could hear them saying, "She just walked away and left them, and this is the result." I thought, the sooner I die, the sooner I can rid myself of all this pain. I thought about my babies in Heaven. I knew that there was a Heaven. And I knew that my babies were with the Lord, but I didn't think God wanted to hear my voice much less hear my prayer. I didn't want to ask him. Why bother God, I'm getting just what I deserve.

My Relief

I had all day and night to think about what I was going to do the next morning. As soon as the opportunity presented itself, I would carry out my plan. My grandma came in with the sleeping pills. I took the pill and it didn't faze me. I listened to my grandma walk across the wooden floors of the house. I knew where she went and where she put the pills. The doctor had told her early to keep them from my sight, because of experiencing so much grief. I was raised in that house, and I knew every crack there was to hide something. As I listened, I knew by her steps that she took the pills into her bedroom and she opened her old squeaky closet door. Then I heard her purse snap closed. I knew where the pills were. This was the only comfort I had felt, since I heard that my girls were no longer with me. The comfort of knowing that I had something to help me end this terrible nightmare was a comfort and relief for me. All I had to do was take the pills and lie back down. Wherever I ended up I would be able to say I couldn't stand life anymore. The place I was going couldn't be as bad as living on earth without my babies.

It was the longest night of my life. This was the first

time that I had been alone. All the people had finally gone home. For the last three days and two nights there had been around the clock a steady flow of people in and out the house. Now it was only my grandma, a nephew, my uncle and me. All the noise was gone, and there was complete silence for the first time. My grandma lived in an old house in the country. All I could do was stare out into the dark shadows of the trees. Oh, I had plenty of memories. I could hear my babies' voices as they ran by the window, playing, laughing, or calling out to me, because one had aggravated the other. I could hear their cry when they would stump their toes. They always loved to go to grandma's house to play. They loved my grandma. We had lain together in this room so many times. My grandma bought an extra bed, so the room would have two beds, my bed from my childhood and the bed that my girls used. Each time Kenny and I would separate, that was where we would sleep. Tonya and Tina in their bed, and Tara would sleep with me, she was the baby and she usually got her way. All that night was filled with memories, regrets, sadness, grief and a river of tears. A steady stream flowed down my cheeks, down my neck and onto the pillow.

My grandma ran a little country store about fifty yards across from her front yard, so I knew her routine. I knew that she opened the store around 7:00 a.m. My grandma had chickens, so the roosters let me know that it wouldn't be long before daylight. Around 6:00 a.m. I heard my grandma's feet hit the floor. She walked from her bedroom straight into my room and softly pushed open my door. I did not move. I had not been asleep all night, and she was checking to see if I was all right. She thought I was asleep. I knew that it was just a matter of time. I thought about how it would be when someone found me. I could hear the things that I thought different people would say. I thought of my girls and the time I had with them here on earth. I was so sad that our time here had ended.

I heard my grandma, getting her little tin moneybox. I heard the store keys jingle. I knew she was getting ready to walk out the door. It would take only a minute to get the pills and get back in bed. My uncle and nephew left early for work. I was finally going to be alone. I heard my grandma walking from her bedroom, keys jingling and across toward my room. She softly pushed the old door open again, to see if I was still all right. She still thought I was sleeping. She knew that I had not slept, so she was careful not to wake me. Pulling the door closed she turned and walked back across the living room to the front door. I heard a knock at the door just as my grandma opened the door. I heard the voice of a woman. The woman said, "I need to see Bonnie". My grandma told her that I was still in bed. She told her that I hadn't had much sleep, and she hated to wake me. I heard a murmur, and then my grandma said, "Let me see if she is awake". I was wondering to myself while they were talking, who in the world was there to see me at that time of the morning. It was only 7:00 a.m. I couldn't believe that someone could be so rude.

My grandma came to the door, pushed it open slowly and called my name in a whisper. She said, "Faye, there is someone here to see you." I asked, "Mama, who is it?" She told me it was Ms. Jane, my seventh grade teacher, who had retired from teaching to answer the call as a missionary there in our county.

My Damascus Road

I slowly lifted myself from the bed. I was so weak. I had not eaten or slept since Friday night. I opened my bedroom door, still in my pajamas, and just looked at her. I didn't know why she would come to visit me so early. She said good morning to me and I quietly said "Hello". She said, "Bonnie, I know it is early, but the Lord sent me over here to tell you that if you would give your heart to him, he would turn your whole life around." As she was talking to me and telling me what God had said, I was thinking to myself, woman you don't know what has happened to me. I have lost all my children, and I am about to end my life. The only thing that is going to help me is to stop breathing. Those were my thoughts as she told me about Jesus, and how Jesus could give me a new life. I had been raised in a Christian home, so I knew there was a God, but I didn't think he wanted to waste his time on me. After all he is the one I thought had punished me by taking my little girls. She continued to talk about Jesus the Son of God and how he could help me. As she talked, I was just staring her in the eyes thinking maybe he could help someone else, but not me. I told her that I had someone in my life, talking about

Bill. She answered quickly, "God will take care of that for you." "But we live together, I said". Again, she answered me quickly saying, "God will work all of that out." She continued to tell me about the love of God. Suddenly, I heard the same voice that I heard on that previous Friday night just as I opened the door. What do you have to lose, Bonnie? I thought of the grief and pain that covered me like a garment. My heart had broken a million times since Friday night. My mind went back to my childhood, when I was two or three years old. My grandma would read me a Bible story early in the morning there in the kitchen doorway, sitting in the sunlight. I remember the pictures of Moses crossing the Red Sea. God did that. The same God she was telling me about then. He was the God that called Lazarus from the dead, and what about all those people he fed in the desert with two fish and five loaves of bread? Those were all miracles. Those were things that were impossible. God did those things that were impossible and this is what Ms. Jane was telling me, that he would do the same for me. What about my children? They were gone and I couldn't stand the thought of that. I couldn't live with all of that grief and pain. Ms. Jane continued. She didn't give up. Again, I heard a voice say, "What do you have to lose Bonnie?" Suddenly, in my mind, I could see myself standing at a crossroad, and I had two ways to go, and it was entirely up to me which way I would go. I could go to the left, and that way was suicide and Hell, or I could go to the right and give God a chance and have Heaven and my babies again. Okay God, I said in my mind, I'm going to give you a chance, and if you are the same God who did those miracles in the Bible, then I will give you a chance to prove yourself right now! Not later, but right now! If you don't prove yourself to me and help me, then I shall die. That was my deal with God. Actually, I was saying, "If you are God, then prove it!"

Ms. Jane quoted John 3:16. "For God so loved the world

that he gave his only begotten son that whosoever shall believe in him shall not perish but have everlasting life." She said, "Bonnie, God sent Jesus here to this earth to die just for you." I had heard this story all of my life and that was all it was to me then, just a story. I remembered all those times I had passed my home church in the past year and turned my head, because I didn't want God to get in my way. I was determined that I was going to run my life, and I didn't need any help. I had tried God before and it seems to me that nothing had changed. Anyway, if he loved me so much why would he let this happen? It seemed that God was "mad" at me instead of in "love" with me.

Again, I heard a voice say to me, "Bonnie, what do you have to lose?" That time I decided to answer the voice I was hearing. This was all taking place in my mind while Ms. Jane was still talking to me. I said," I don't have anything to lose." I held my head up and looked into Ms. Jane's eyes and said okay, quietly. "Will you come with me into my Grandma's bedroom?" She followed me and I closed the door and began to cry. To be honest with you, I didn't think that it was going to work.

Ms. Jane told me that she was going to lead me in the sinner's prayer. She did not ask me to lift my hands, but I remember I lifted my hands and stretched them as far as I could. She asked me to repeat after her and I did. This is the prayer I prayed:

> God I come to you in the name of Jesus,
> I need you God in my life,
> I have come before you this beautiful
> morning to give myself to you,
> Take my life Lord and take full control of it,
> I am a sinner Lord,
> Please forgive me Lord of all my sins.

Truthfully, from the moment I said "Forgive me Lord of my sins, I felt the weight of the world lift off me. I could see as I looked up the feeling of grief take wings and fly. The feelings of guilt took wings and flew away. The feelings of sadness took wings, and by that time I was screaming to the top of my voice. "I'm saved! I'm saved!" I started running out the front door at 7:15 a.m., into the front yard and out into the middle of the road still screaming, "I'm saved! I'm saved!" I looked at the trees, and it was if they were clapping their leaves together, praising God with me. Everything looked so different. Everything I saw was beautiful. The tears were still falling, but they were different tears. They were tears of joy. I don't think I had ever experienced crying tears of joy in my whole life, but it sure felt good. I ran down the road to my mother's home and opened the front door. I woke everyone in the house and probably everyone in the neighborhood shouting from the top of my voice. "I'm saved! I'm saved!"

I was amazed at the difference that prayer and God's touch made in my life. It was a miracle. I had just received a miracle from God. The same God of the Bible that did all those awesome things for people had just come into my grandma's bedroom and touched me. I was different! I knew I was different. I could feel the difference. I would look at my hands, and they seemed so clean and pure, I didn't understand everything that had happened to me, but I can tell you this. I knew that God had just saved me. I also knew it happened within a matter of seconds. No longer than it takes to say, "Forgive me of my sins" I was a different woman.

Psalms 116:8, "For thou has delivered my soul from death, mine eyes from tears and my feet from falling."

Acts 2:21, "And it shall come to pass, that whosoever shall call on the name of the Lord shall be saved."

Then I could say that I knew the God of the Bible. I had an encounter with the same God, which created the Heavens and earth. I knew then just what King David meant when he said, "God had delivered my soul from death," because I was at Hell's door when God showed up at my front door. My tears he wiped away with his own hand, and my feet; he planted on the Solid Rock. Praise God!

I called upon the name of Jesus, and he saved me. I was a new creation. Old things passed away and behold all things were new. For this there wasn't enough praise. I was different. I would go into the bathroom, lock the door and just stare into the mirror. I was beside myself with the change that Jesus had made in me, and I knew the change was real. There wasn't anyone who could tell me any different. I was there before he saved me, when he saved me and after he saved me. This was the hand of God without a doubt.

Four days after the funeral, people were still coming by to pay their respects, but instead of finding a mother full of grief and pain, they found a brand new Bonnie. There was such a difference that God had made in me that my family was really concerned about me. They couldn't accept what had happened as simply being the hand of God. They thought I had completely lost my mind. One minute I was engulfed in grief and pain and the next minute I was a different person. That couldn't be. I thought it was funny when my family called the doctor to tell him what had happened. The doctor told my grandmother that she should take me to a psychiatrist. I reminded my grandmother of how she told me about the God of the Bible and his son, Jesus, and how he performed the impossible. Then I asked her if she believed the miracles God performed in the Bible and recorded, that we would know that nothing is impossible. After all, I had just two days earlier laid my little girls in their graves. All I knew was that I was dying with grief and sadness and now I was looking forward to the day that I would be reunited with my girls. I knew that I could live in this life until that blessed day happened.

New Creation

There was a tremendous change in my life. It was only a few days until I realized that I had changed, but others had not. I was happy, full of the joy of the Lord. The Lord had given me a smile instead of tears. He had given me the tongue of praise, a hope for the future in this life and eternity. He had forgiven all of my sins. I felt like a new woman, because of the hand of God. I walked as a new woman. God totally transformed me, and I was excited! Nobody could tell me differently. God was real, and he had, through his grace and mercy come to me when I was in the pit with no hope. The change was too much for some, and others just didn't believe it. They said it was all an act. Others said it wouldn't last long. But I knew in my heart what God had done for me. When I could have died and gone to Hell, He saved me! When I would hear the things that people in the community were saying about me I couldn't believe them. Everyone had an opinion about the death of my children. The majority of the community labeled me as the mom who left her children, now they were dead, and I was GUILTY.

James 3:8, "But the tongue can no man tame; it is an unruly evil, full of deadly poison." I was pumped full of deadly poison. I was a newborn babe in Christ, and I didn't know how to protect myself from those fiery darts. As I would hear the things people were saying about me, I would take a trip down to my little soul chest and pack. I would pack the words spoken against me, and the opinions of others, deep inside. Each time I visited, I would pack the guilty verdict that almost everyone had me labeled with deep inside. I knew what I had to do, just hold my head up and keep walking, no matter what the people thought or said about me. I knew in whom I had believed. So I just kept walking and loving my Lord.

What about the death of my children? Didn't I miss them? I did miss them terribly with all of my heart, but I knew I had to keep going, pressing for the mark of the high calling. I had my eyes on eternity. I knew that I had to give Jesus my all. I remembered the night that I received the knock at the door, and on the way to open the door I heard a voice say to me, "I have them now." That was the voice of Jesus.

John 10:9, "I am the door: by me if any man enter in, he shall be saved, and shall go in and out and find pasture." I had this confidence in the power of my God. I knew he would carry me through. He had promised me in his word that he would never leave me or forsake me. His word had sustained me. I fell in love with the word. The word is a lamp unto my feet and light to my path. The word of God was the most exciting thing that I had ever discovered. The more I heard the word of God, the greater my knowledge became about how much God loved me.

I would stay up until the wee hours of the morning reading and seeking to know him more. I remembered as a little girl the stories my grandma had told me, and the ones I had learned in Sunday school. There were so many that I had never heard and I marveled at the work of God's hand. Reading his word gave me strength. I had become a witness of the mighty power of God. I would read of the mighty works that he did back through the ages, and then looked at my own life, and I could see his work in my life. I knew without a doubt, that the God of Abraham, Isaac, and Jacob had sent the missionary worker to me in the darkest hour of my life and rescued me from destruction.

Two months later I heard a man on the radio by the name of Shambach. I would listen to him every day. Then I heard a man by the name of Charles Capps, then Kenneth Hagen's and Kenneth Copeland. These great men of God became and would be my teachers for the next twenty years.

I was growing in the word of God. I was seeing and learning things that I had never been taught. I found out that the Bible was more than just a book. It was a book that was ALIVE. Through the teachings of these great men of God, I learned how to apply the word of God to my life.

I was very lonely. I had started a new job and that took up some of my time, but I was used to taking care of three children. Now my free time was spent studying the word of God. My family was concerned that I was spending too much time in the Bible, but I knew who had saved my life and how important it was to stay connected to my life-giving source.

John 8:32, "You shall know the truth and the truth shall set you free." I couldn't afford to get stuck in the mud of religion, so I kept my eyes focused on Jesus and his word, and he led me in the straight paths.

I was in love with the Lord. I had the inner peace of knowing that I had found the source of all life, Jesus the Son of the Living God. I couldn't praise him enough! For the first time I was enjoying life. I was learning about Jesus and the salvation that he bought and paid for, just for me, and knowing that I had found the most important thing in life-Jesus, who is the giver of life. I was astonished at how the word of God would leap out at me and speak words of healing to my heart. He had worked in me a healing that only he could have done. I was a walking miracle and no one knew it better than I.

Three weeks after the accident, the search for my oldest daughter was called off. They had searched the river for miles downstream and had found nothing. There was nothing I could do. I walked down the railroad tracks day by day looking for my baby, but to no avail. I knew that I was going to have to lay this pain of losing her body at the feet of Jesus. I couldn't carry the burden.

Six months later on a Tuesday afternoon around 6:30 p.m., I was working on a swing shift. My supervisor asked me to go with him to his office. I had no idea what was going on. Actually, I thought it was concerning my job performance. We entered his office and he told me that he hated to be the one to tell me, but the authorities had found a body. Truthfully, there were tears, but very few. I had cut off all emotion. I felt the hurt and pain, but it was as if I had commanded my heart not to grieve. I did not want to feel that awful pain called grief again. I just wanted to love God and keep going forward. I didn't ever want to look back. When I arrived at my grandma's house, there again, I saw the cars gathered down both sides of the road. I realized that I would again walk down that road of burying my baby.

I was in love with the word of God. It brought peace to my soul.

Psalm 119:116,117, David said, "Uphold me according to thy word, that I may live: and let me not be ashamed of my hope. Hold me up, and I shall be safe: and I will have respect unto thy statutes continually." The word of God was my hope and strength.

Around two months after the accident, I found the scripture Mark 11:24. "Whatsoever thing you desire when you pray you shall have them." Now, being a new baby in Christ and a mother who had not seen the body of her little girl. It was very hard for me to accept that she was not coming back. After I found this scripture it was easier to believe God for the impossible. I prayed and said, "Lord God of Heaven and of earth I know that nothing is impossible with you, and your word tells me that I can have whatsoever I desire; and I am a witness to your miraculous power. I also know that it will not be long before you are coming back to get your saints. You have said Lord that you are going to show your power and your glory here in this earth before that time and I ask that you let your glory be seen here. I thank you for it Lord." Brother Kenneth Copeland had taught me well, how to ask and receive. Well, there was nothing for me to do, but believe and wait. I want you to know this was from the bottom of my heart. I really believed that God would honor my request, and bring my little girl back to me, therefore; I expected a miracle to happen.

I had experienced the power of God when he came into my life that day in my grandma's bedroom, so I didn't have any problem believing. I knew that if he could lift me up out of the terrible pit that I was in, he could do anything.

So the next thing I had to do according to II Corinthians 4:13 was to believe: "I believe, and therefore I have spoken; we believe, and therefore speak." The next thing I would do concerning this request I asked of the Lord was to tell someone my faith. I knew I had to speak it and this would be the thing that would cause people to think I had fallen off the cliff.

I stood up one Sunday morning in church, boldly proclaiming that the congregation would witness the return of my daughter. I didn't know how God would do it, but I knew he would do it. Now, I don't have to tell you that when I made that proclamation, the whole church got silent.

"Another Holy Hush moment".

I did not stop believing that God was going to give my daughter back. I had to tell someone else. Someone I thought that was important. I went into my plant manager's office and proclaimed my faith to him. I said, "Mr. Quick, I have come in here to tell you about something that is going to happen and when it comes to pass, you will know that only the hand of God performed the miracle. Then I said, "My little girl is coming back home!" God is going to do a miracle. Mr. Quick knew about the accident. He started sweating. He looked at me as if to say, this poor child has lost her mind. Then I thanked him for listening to me. He said in a nervous voice, "Thank you for telling me." Then I walked out.

I believed for a miracle and if it took looking crazy, then so be it. Word spread quickly around the community about Bonnie believing that her child was coming back home. They talked about how I thought I would receive a miracle like those in the Bible. I don't have to tell you, I was the talk of the county, and all the church folks were buzzing.

My grandma and others tried to talk to me about the reality of it all, but I refused to let anyone's opinion touch the vision I had of my little girl coming home. To me, God's word had settled it.

When my supervisor gave me the news about my daughter being located, he offered to take me home. I told him that I would be fine. I left work and went to this lake, where I enjoyed visiting to have quiet time with the Lord. This was where I chose to go before going to my grandma's house where I knew I would see all the people whom I had professed my faith. At my favorite place, as I sat quietly before the Lord, I asked him what happened. I reminded him that I had believed him and his word. "What happened, Lord?" I asked. By this time, I had broken into tears. I picked up a stick and threw it toward Heaven and said, "Lord why didn't you give me my baby back?" I know it would not have been a problem for you to have performed a miracle and brought my baby back. I fell down to my knees and sobbed. The Holy Spirit came and surrounded me with his comfort and love. He assured me that he had seen my faith and that it pleased him, but bringing back my little girl was not part of his plan.

I got into my car and went to my grandma's house. There were a lot of people waiting for me to arrive. I had decided on the way home that I would be strong. I did not realize how many loads of pain, hurt and disappointment I would unload in my little soul chest. When I visited my soul chest then, instead of opening it up and making a deposit, I packed to get it all in. You see I didn't understand casting down vain imaginations according to II Corinthians 10:5. What I would do instead of casting down. I would push the feelings deep into my soul. I had decided that I would serve God no matter what. Job 13:15 states: "Though he slay me, yet will I trust him." He was still God to me. He didn't have to prove anything.

Goodbye Again

The day of the funeral for my oldest daughter, I was already seated when Kenny arrived. We had made it through the first funeral without communicating. That time Kenny chose to be seated at the opposite end of the tent. It was a graveside service. I sat there motionless through the service. I wanted to get it over and go on with God. By the time the funeral was over, no less than thirty minutes, again I had somehow turned my emotions off. I had commanded my inner self to refrain from crying. There would be no more tears, or grief, or sadness. I had decided that if I was going to live, I would live with my emotions under lock and key and only I would have the key. Underneath the locked emotions was my soul chest. I had a lot of baggage, and it was all hurt and pain in one form or another.

My walk with the Lord is, and always will be a process. I was a baby in Christ, loving him and learning about him. I did not know what to do with the hurt and pain that I was experiencing, in addition to the words and opinions of others. Everyone boasted his or her judgmental opinions concerning whose fault it was and who was to blame. I felt as if I had a sign engraved on my back and I could not get it off. Guilty! God had relieved me once of the guilt but when it raised its ugly head again, I did not know what to do with it, so I just kept packing the pain deeper into my little soul chest and locking the door to my emotions. The words that were spoken against me were so hurtful for me. I had a friend who felt that it was only right that she keep me informed with the latest news. She would tell me who said it and every word that was spoken. If I had only known what I know today concerning God's life-giving word, but I didn't, and my Lord kept me through it all. I give him all the glory! God has been faithful in every area of my life. I will say of the Lord, he is my refuge and my fortress: my God; in him I will trust.

A Wonderful Husband

It would not be long until I would put the word of God to the test. I had learned how to ask and believe God for the desires of my heart. One night while coming home from work, I started telling God why I thought I needed a husband.

Isaiah 1:18, "Come now, let us reason together saith the Lord."

I would go to the Lord in prayer and conversation and present my reasons to him. The teaching of my home church where I was raised was that you could not get married again, if you had been previously divorced. That was their teaching and not the word of God. I would not be conformed to their traditions and religion. When their rules said no pants for women, I wore my pants. They said no makeup, I was the one lifting holy hands with red nails and praising him with painted lips. I didn't do this out of a rebellious spirit, but I knew that I was free and in perfect liberty. I remember my grandma said to me one day, "I will be glad when the Lord sanctifies you, and takes that nail polish off your fingers". My grandma just spoke her mind. I loved her so much.

So one night I prayed, Father I thank you for your presence, thank you so much for your great love upon me, but Father I sure would like to have a husband. I know Father that you don't want us to be lonely and alone in this world. I also know that your grace is sufficient to carry me, but I would like to have a good husband. I told the Lord what kind of husband I wanted. A good- hearted man, Lord, one that will love me with all of his heart. A husband, my heart can trust. I know you have the perfect husband for me father. I am going to wait on you. Then I thanked him for a good husband every day.

Eight months later (while at work) I saw this handsome man, which I had not seen before. Because our company was large, with so many employees, there were a lot of people that I had not seen. There was something different about this man. .

The next night at work I secretly looked for him, but did not see him. Just before time to go home I was standing around "looking busy". I wasn't thinking about this man. I looked up, and he was standing in front of me. I felt my face turn red. He asked my name, and we introduced ourselves. We smiled because of our similar names. Donnie and Bonnie. So we had our first date. After the date, I went home and told the Lord that I would very much like to have Donnie as a part of my life. I asked the Lord to show me in a dream, whether or not he was the promised one. I went to sleep and dreamed that I was standing at the church altar with my hand in his hand. I awoke in awe of how God answered me, and how the dream had come. I knew without a doubt that he was my husband from the Lord. God gave so much more than I could ever ask or think when he gave Donnie to me. He is truly God-sent. He is the other part of me that makes me complete. I could never thank God enough. He knew whom I needed. What a precious gift from Heaven. He led us and we grew together as a family serving the Lord and daily giving our lives to him. Psalm 92:2

states: "I will say of the Lord, he is my refuge and fortress: my God in whom I will trust."

Six months later, Donnie proposed to me and of course, I said yes. We were and are a match made in Heaven. God provides. Donnie is my true love; we have the "Agape" love of God. (Unconditional Love). Genesis 2:24, "and they shall become one." He was and is my true friend. Again, I was a witness of the promises of God's Word. He showed himself strong by giving me a wonderful husband. We were married May 8, 1981.

On February 2, 1983, God so graciously gave us a son. I prayed and asked the Lord for another opportunity to become a mother. Again, he honored my request. I had asked the Lord for a baby boy. I told the Lord, that I didn't want another girl, because I didn't want to compare. The Lord is so good. He gave us a son whose name is Chezz. He has been a blessing to both of us. I promised the Lord if he would allow me to be a mother again, I would raise my child to know him. 1 Samuel 1:27,28 states: "For this child I prayed; and the Lord hath given me my petition, which I asked of him: Therefore also I have lent him to the Lord; as long as he liveth he shall be lent to the Lord."

The Pain In My Chest

The pain would not go away. In October 1987, a vicious pain awakened me in my chest. I thought I was having a heart attack. The pain was unbearable. I woke my husband, Donnie, and he sat me up in a chair. Finally, the pain eased enough for me to get back into bed. I didn't know what had happened. It felt as if something had exploded in my chest. As I lay there, unable to sleep, I could feel the pain increasing again, and by morning the pain was unbearable. I can't begin to tell you what I went through because of the pain that would not go away.

From October 1987 through May 1994, I went to see seventeen specialists, nine psychiatrists, six general physicians, five plastic surgeons, two chiropractors, four pain clinics, had one heart catherization. Also, I had six nerve blocks to the area that was hurting. Each one did extensive tests from head to toe searching for the pain. I thought I would literally die. In fact, the pain was so intensive and intolerable, I asked the Lord to please end my life. I had felt the unbearable heart pain when I lost my girls and now I was feeling unbearable pain in my physical body. I was useless to everyone. My dear husband and my son Chezz catered to my every need. The only diagnosis that I received from any doctor was a severe case of depression. I disputed them until the end. I refused to believe my problem was depression. All of the doctors found out about the loss of my children. They zeroed in on the accident as the cause of depression. They told Donnie that the pain was caused by grief. They said this had happened because I had never properly grieved and my body was reacting to the grief that was locked up inside me. This was unacceptable to me. I knew I had a physical pain in my chest, and it was not mental. I did not need to grieve because Jesus had healed me. That had always been my testimony. I didn't understand why God would allow this terrible thing to happen to me. There were times when I thought God was punishing me, but I didn't understand why. Satan would come with his lies. He would tell me that my suffering was because of the accident. He would tell me it came from God.

Dr. Toney, one of the psychiatrists, in his conclusion said, "Surely this woman is dying of a broken heart, because of the death of her children." He told my husband that I needed to be admitted to the hospital so they I could receive twenty-four hour care. They told me the grief of the loss of my girls had to be released, or I would probably end up hurting myself. I did not agree with them at all. I didn't know what the pain was coming from, but I did know that it wasn't the death of my girls.

In May 1994, we traveled to Texas. I had heard of a doctor that might be able to help me. Within fifteen minutes, that doctor had found the origin of that long, torturous pain. I knew God would come through for me, but this time I felt he had taken his precious time. I thank you Lord for relief! It was a long and painful seven years.

In March 1982, I had had surgery for silicone implants. In October 1987, the night that I felt the explosion in my chest, was the night the right implant ruptured. The second time, the explosion was on the left side of my upper chest. It happened on Christmas Day around 3:00 p.m. I was resting when I felt the same pain that I had experienced four years earlier. That pain was not as intense as the first episode.

The doctors and tests did not find my problem. I have asked myself the question so my times. All the doctors checked me and did every x-ray and test that was available, but they found nothing wrong with the implants. The surgery that should have taken 45 – 60 minutes took four hours. The implants had grown into the tissue of my body and the doctor said, "It was a mess to remove."

Later on I would be able to see how God used this problem in my life to get to my soul. I know now at this time of my life, that God has his ways of reaching us. The next road of my life planned by God, would prove to be most difficult.

My walk with the Lord was a strong one. I continued through the years loving God with all my heart, teaching my son to love God with all his heart and loving my precious husband with all that was within me. We had a very special love for each other. God has blessed our love with his love. I thank God every day for the gift of my husband and son. I am very blessed!

However, there was one thing bothering me. I was finding myself thinking about my girls more and more. It seemed as though someone had found my little soul chest and left the door open. I couldn't close it back no matter how hard I tried. Seventeen years had passed since the death of my girls. I think the terrible experience of pain in my chest and explaining the accident over and over to all the doctors had opened the door to my soul, and God, being so merciful and so good, would not allow me to close it again. He loved me so much that he allowed pain to come, so I could be freed from the captivity of my little soul chest.

Jeremiah 30:16 states: "Therefore all they that devour thee shall be devoured; and all thine adversaries, every one of them shall go into captivity; and they that spoil thee shall be a spoil, and all that prey upon thee will give a prey."

The Lord had given me this scripture so many times in the past seventeen years since the death of my children. God continued to send me this word, that he would free me of all captivity. "Now I understand Lord," I thought.

The Prophet

The prophet came and God was with him. There was a man of God who came to our church for a three-night revival. He had the gift of prophecy. He called for the prayer line to be formed, and I was one of about twenty who got in the line for prayer. When he started to pray for each one, a word of prophecy would come forth. I was in the center of the line. When it was my turn to be prayed for, the prophet just passed me by and went to the next person. I knew that he had seen me, so I started asking God what was going on. I told God how I hoped that he had not told his prophet anything personal about me. The prophet continued to pray until he had prayed for the last one in line. Then he turned and came back to stand in front of me. He stared into my face, and I was wondering what he was going to say. He very boldly opened his mouth and said, "God said you need to offer someone a peace offering." He asked me if I knew who he was talking about. I didn't want to embarrass him by saying "No" so I said "Yes". I really did not have a clue as to whom he was talking about. I did not know of anyone that I owed an apology. I guess he could see in my eyes that I was searching my heart to find that someone God was talking about. He said, "God said when you offer this someone in your life a peace offering God, is going to show up at your house." Then he asked, "Do you know whom God is talking about?" Again, I said, "Yes." I still did not have a clue. He asked me once more if I was sure I knew whom God was talking about? This time when I answered, "Yes" it was as if the Spirit of God opened up a casket inside my soul and out came Kenny's face. It was his face from the last time; I had seen him at the gravesite of our oldest daughter, Tonya. After I realized what God was saying to me, I broke down into tears of sorrow, because I realized that I had unforgiveness in my heart toward Kenny all those years. I repented before God and asked the Lord to open the door for me to see him, and I would offer the apology or peace offering to him.

I remember that hot summer Sunday evening at the funeral of our oldest daughter, Kenny and I sat through the burial of all three of our girls, blaming one another, and parting without even a glance. We both had left without mending anything. It was a terrible tragedy that neither of us wanted to be reminded of.

The Plan

The next day I sought the Lord on the plan to allow me to speak with Kenny. I had probably passed him on the road three times in the past seventeen years. There had been absolutely no contact. None! Now the Lord was telling me to go offer him a peace offering or apologize to him. I knew that this would be a job for God and not me. I was willing to offer the peace branch, but I didn't have the slightest idea of how it was going to happen. The first thing I would do was to tell my husband, Donnie, that I needed to see Kenny and why. He agreed that it would be okay. I have a wonderful and understanding husband. I sent word to Kenny and he refused to meet with me, so, I came up with plan two. I would write him a letter and that is what I did. The messenger that I sent came back to me and said, "Mail delivered," and "Mail accepted", that part was accomplished. The next thing would be, "God was going to show up at my house." I was so excited. I had waited for so many years for the dream of my ministry to come to the fullness of time. I knew God had given me the gift of teaching. I had been teaching in the church for many years, but God had promised me many years ago that he would use me in the last days of harvest and I felt I was ready. I had waited for seventeen years. I never could understand why God would not release me into the ministry. But then God had promised to show up at my house, if I obeyed his prophet, and I obeyed fully. Nothing left to do, but wait for the Lord to show up.

In the meantime, I was feeling emotions that I did not understand. I was having nightmares about my little girls. That was so unusual, because it had been seventeen years since their accident, and I had been doing just fine. I may have dreamed about my girls three times in those seventeen years. I did not know what was going on, but I did know that something was not right.

In the next three months, which followed, my emotions would unleash. Until then I had not cried or grieved about anything. It had been seventeen years since I commanded my emotions to shut down. I did not understand what I had done to myself. I found it hard to cry over anything no matter how sad the situation. There weren't any tears for me. I remember so many times saying to the Lord, "Why can't I cry?" My mind would always go back to the death of my girls, but I still did not understand why.

I knew something was wrong, but I was refusing to believe it was the death of my children. How could that be? God had been my strength and would continue to strengthen me. One day there was a phone call from a dear sister in the Lord from my church. She wanted to share a dream that she had about me the night before. I knew in my heart that God was about to speak to me in a dream. She said, "I dreamed that you were laying on your couch in your living room, and your house was very, very clean. When I walked into your home, there were children playing in the other rooms of your home, and you were begging me to please stop the children from playing so that you could rest." Then she explained that she felt it was really important for her to share this dream with me.

I asked the Lord what he saying to me. I did not want to think about the death of my girls having an effect on me. I had confessed healing from that terrible accident and that confession was my stronghold. The Lord had helped me through all these years, and I wasn't about to think that he was going to change. His word had held me up, and his word would continue to be my help. All the times the psychiatrists said, it wasn't natural for a mother not to grieve, I would respond that; God had healed me of all the grief and pain. They always stressed that one-day it would come out, and I would just laugh to myself and say, "They don't know the God I serve!"

When I asked the Lord what the dream meant he gave me this scripture.

Jeremiah 31:15, "Thus saith the Lord; a voice was heard in Ramah, lamentation, and bitter weeping; Rachel weeping for her children refused to be comforted for her children, because they were not." I said, "Lord, please don't talk to me about my children. Father, please don't remind me. I just want you to take these feelings of sorrow and regret away. Lord, I just want to go forward, Father." The only conversation I wanted to have with God concerning my girls was to praise him for their eternal home, and thank him for saving me and healing me of all the grief and pain. I didn't want to listen to anything concerning my girls' death. This could be also, the angel of light trying to get me off the straight and narrow road, 2 Corinthians 11:14,15. Anyway God had promised that he was coming to my house. I made a decision to pray and seek the Lord concerning this matter.

I sought the Lord and he gave me scripture from Jeremiah 30:12,13, "for thus saith the Lord, thy bruise is incurable, and thy wound is grievous. There is none to plead thy cause that thou mayest be bound up: thou has no healing medicines."

The Lord was saying to me, that all the hurt and pain

that I had in my little soul chest was a continuous hurt, and there was no one to help. There was no medicine, nothing to help Bonnie but God. It was a sorrow to my soul, and he wanted me to admit that my little soul chest needed to be emptied and cleaned. Again, I turned a deaf ear to the Lord! I did not want to go there. The dreams were happening more frequently by this time. Each time I dreamed about my precious little girls, someone was trying to keep them away from me. I would try so hard to get them, but I could never reach them. I would awaken with a broken heart. None of those bad thoughts and dreams started until God asked me to offer a peace offering to Kenny.

I was finding myself drained of my natural strength. I was losing interest in everything. All I wanted to do was cry, and I tried so hard day after day to hold back the tears. I was active in my church. I knew I had to be faithful in the area God had placed me. There were many times I would wear a smile that wasn't really there. I was really feeling sad, and I began to look back and mourn silently while living on the outside as a "strong woman of faith". I walked that walk with perfection, but inside I knew something was desperately wrong.

I thank God for my pastor and his wonderful wife. They were God-sent to me for such a time as then and now. I knew I had to talk to someone, and that someone could only be my pastor's wife. God has given her much wisdom. She is my spiritual mother, and I knew she could point me in the right direction. I made an appointment with her, and I began to tell her of all the things that were going on inside me. We prayed together, and the Holy Spirit filled the room. It was such a gentle, loving spirit. I rejoiced in his presence. I remember my spiritual mother saying to me, "Bonnie, maybe God has waited until now to completely heal you of the pain of losing your girls, and maybe God waited until you were mature enough in Him to heal you of that great loss." She continued, "Maybe God has been carrying you, and now he wants you to walk on your own."

I received my healing from God that day and was ready to go forth in the Lord. But little did I know that God had just introduced me to the road that I would walk down the next three years. I continued to wear the face of a "got-it-all together Christian" when inside I felt as if I were dying with sorrow. One Sunday morning our pastor's wife presented the message for the morning service. I will never forget that powerful sermon. The sermon was entitled "Who's Breathing on You?" You would have had to been there to understand. I felt like God had his hand on my soul pressing down and would not let up. The Lord spoke to me and said, "Bonnie, who are you allowing to Breathe on you?" I could not sit still. All I wanted to do was to get out of there. I didn't know what God was up to, but I was losing strength fast.

God Had A Plan

It was a three-night layman revival and my pastor's wife called me to ask if I would be willing to speak one night. I told her that I would pray and seek God and get back with her. As I was seeking God, He spoke to me and said, "Bonnie, I want you to give your testimony about the accident and how you met me." I was so excited to hear the Lord say that to me. I had waited for seventeen years. I wanted to give my testimony, but the Lord would not release me to do so. I questioned him so many times about it. I would ask the Lord why he would not allow me to tell how He came down and saved me from such grief and misery. I told him that my testimony was just as touching as other people testimony, but the Lord had never released me to tell my story until then. Praise God!

I knew that God was really going to show up. Finally, he was going to release me into the ministry. That had to be the time and season for me to step out into my calling.

The theme song that night was "Look What the Lord has done!" I was so excited and nervous. I had told my testimony to very few people, and now I would finally get to shout it from the housetop! I could finally tell just what God had done for me.

The night of the service I began by telling the people how Jesus came to the disciples in the storm. Mark 6:48. They were in a windstorm and Jesus went where they were. He didn't wait until they "called" out to him. He saw that they were in trouble and he went to them. I also told them about the woman whose only son was dead. This lady wasn't screaming out to Jesus for help. Jesus saw the funeral procession and went to her and raised her son from the dead.

Then I began to tell how Jesus came to me in the storm of my life. I began by telling the story of the car accident and how Jesus came to me when I had no will to live. I had no hope of ever living a life in this world without my children. It was impossible for my mind to grasp that thought. I told them how God had given me a reason to live. I explained to them how the Love of God had sustained me through all the years and his word had lead me and kept me. I gave God all the glory!

The congregation gave me their full attention, and they were very receptive to my testimony. They gave a standing ovation when I finished. God had really showed up and showed off. To God be the glory! When I sat down, my pastor gave an altar call for those that needed God's touch in their lives. There were many that went forward that night.

Something is Wrong!

When I sat down I was trembling. I didn't feel right. I felt as if I wanted to start running and never stop. I leaned over to my husband, Donnie and said, "I must leave!" He asked me why I wanted to leave, I told him I didn't know, but I felt I had to get out of there. Donnie told me that I could not leave at that time. We would have to wait until the pastor dismissed everyone. He said, "We just can't walk out!" I agreed, but inside, emotions were coming up, and I was unable to control them. So many people came up to me and said how much my testimony had touched them. All I wanted to do was get in the car and go home. Driving home it was silent in the car. Donnie very gently asked me what was wrong. "God really used you tonight honey." he said. I replied, "Well, I guess everyone knows me now!" I explained to Donnie that I felt as if my whole life had been opened up for everyone to see. I felt naked and ashamed.

The next day I felt as though I had traveled back in time. Thoughts were returning, thoughts I hadn't had since I had given my life to Jesus. The same day I had an appointment with a new doctor. He was going through my record and said, "I see you have had severe depression for a long time."

I replied, "No sir, I have not." Then I began telling him about the pain in my chest situation. He didn't want to hear about the pain. He said, "I only go by what is in your record, and your record tells me that you are suffering, from severe depression." I very politely stood up and said, "Thank you for your time," and walked out. I got into my car and started telling God how I was fed up with people telling me that I was depressed. I had lived the last seventeen years just fine! I fussed to myself and to God all the way home. I told him how I wanted this whole deal with the grief and sorrow to end. My greatest desire was to go forward in God and fulfill his plan and purpose for my life. I then said, "Lord, please remove from me all of the past that may still be in me, and Lord if I am depressed, you show me." I didn't realize what I asked God for.

God Put Me Down

When I returned home I started cooking dinner for Donnie. I was still complaining to the Lord about the doctor's comment. Again, I said, "If I am depressed, then Lord you show me." As soon as those words, which came from my mouth, I saw (in the spirit) God's hand come down and in his hand was a baby-sitting in the center of his hand. Then I saw God tilt his hand and put the toddler down. The toddler started crying and saying, "I don't want to walk, I don't want to walk!" I knew that God was putting me down. I said to the Lord, "Please don't put me down. "I can't walk by myself." I suddenly realized that God had carried me all those years. God reminded me of the poem "Footprint in the Sand." I began to cry, begging God not to put me down. I asked him how I would make it if he put me down. "I thought you had healed me Lord, and besides all that, I am afraid to walk by myself." I told him I didn't think I could make it by myself. I continued to make my complaint to the Lord, and tell him that I did not understand why he was doing this to me. It seemed so unfair. I had always given God all the glory and honor for coming to me when my babies had died. I felt like God was doing me wrong. It seemed so cruel.

Spiritually, I was in trouble for the first time in seventeen years. I didn't know what God was up to, but it didn't look easy to me. I was in a place of pain again, where no one could reach me. I would ask the Lord, "Why now?" It had been so many years ago. "Why do you keep pressing the issue, Lord?" I asked. I told the Lord how I was fine until he told me he was going to show up at my house. I didn't understand why I must face the death of my babies again. I somehow knew God would ask me to visit that time in my past, and I did not want to go there. I was afraid I would not be able to return. I was afraid I would be engulfed in grief. The thought of going back to the death of my girls was unbearable.

I was falling into a deep depression. I couldn't eat or sleep. I had lost thirteen pounds in two weeks. All I could do was cry. It was as if all the tears of seventeen years came out like a river. Donnie was very concerned. He would lay his hand on me and pray for God to strengthen me. He didn't understand what was going on either, but we both trusted God for his faithfulness to help me. It was getting hard for me to deny that nothing was wrong. I knew something was terribly wrong. I didn't know how to handle the load of grief that had attacked my soul. Again, I was in another "trust God or die" situation. I had known nothing but God for the past seventeen years. I didn't understand why God would lead me down this road to healing.

Since I had given my testimony, everything had fallen apart. I was dealing with all these emotions, and doing all that I could to hold myself together. I was hoping and praying that God would come soon and deliver my soul.

A Visit From God

I was sitting in my recliner seeking God, praying that he would change his mind. I had been desperately seeking God and praying. I heard the Spirit of God speak to my heart and say, "I'm coming to your house, Bonnie." I remember my heart started beating fast. I wanted God to show up, but I didn't know what he might require of me when he came. I heard again the Lord's voice (in my spirit) saying, "I am coming to your house, Bonnie." Well, that time I turned and peeked out the shade of my window down the road that led to my house. That was a habit I had. We live about a quarter of a mile from the main road, and the road that leads to my house is a small winding dirt road. Around the curve of that dirt road, I saw (in my spirit) a vision of God coming on this huge backhoe tractor. I mean the backhoe that I saw was a monster. It was running full speed. I dropped the shade and started pleading with God. Lord! Don't come to my house. Please don't come, Lord. The spirit of the Lord spoke to me and said, "We are going to dig up your past and get it settled once and for all, so you can go forward." I knew God had promised to come show up at my house, but I wasn't expecting him to come for that reason.

When I stopped crying, I asked the Lord what was wrong with me. I opened my Bible and my eyes landed on this scripture. Jeremiah 15:9, "A mother of seven sickens and faints, for all her sons are dead. Her sun is gone down while it is yet day. She sits childless now, disgraced for all her children have been killed." (Living Bible) I could not remember ever reading this scripture. It was overwhelming to me that God would answer me so directly. He said, "Bonnie, I have been carrying you, and now I want you to let me heal you completely, so you can help others". The Lord said, "Bonnie, if I had not picked you up when your girls left, you wouldn't have lived. I carried you until you were strong enough to handle the death of your children." That scripture told me what I had been carrying all that time. I understood that scripture. I knew that I was sick with grief, and I was getting weaker; because of the death of my girls. (Her sun has gone down while it is yet day). This was the deep depression that covered my soul. (She sits childless now, disgraced for all her children have been killed). This was all the guilt that I felt when I lost my girls and the disgrace part. I felt so ashamed when I gave my testimony. I understood, then, the shameful feelings that had imprisoned me.

The Lord had previously given me this scripture: Jeremiah 13:12-15. "For your sins an incurable bruise, a terrible wound. There is no one to help you or to bind up your wound and no medicine does any good. All your lovers have left you; they don't care anything about you any more. For I have wounded you cruelly, as though I was your enemy; for your sins are so many, your guilt is so great, why do you protest your punishment? Your sin is so scandalous that your sorrow should never end. It is because your guilt is great, and I have to punish you so much".

The Lord was telling me that this was how I felt inside about myself because, I had left my children, and they lost their lives in the accident. I had all those years blamed Bonnie in my subconscious. She was the only one who was guilty, and there was no medicine that could help me. I felt that everyone blamed me and that no one wanted anything to do with me. All the punishment in the world wasn't enough for me. This was a lot to carry, and I didn't realize I was carrying this load.

This is the guilt I carried for seventeen years, and I had no idea all of this was inside my soul. I knew I had packed a lot of hurt, but I did not know I had all of that inside me. I lived my life as if everything was fine. God continued to give me that word concerning the condition of my soul. He had put me down to walk on my own, but he was not going to walk away and leave me. He was going to walk beside me until everything that I had buried was uncovered and dealt with. All the guilt, pain, sorrow, grief and depression had to go. Psalms 40:2, "He brought me up also out of a horrible pit, out of the miry clay, and set my feet upon a rock, and established my goings." I knew he would do the same for me. I had learned through the years how to take God's word for what it was, HIS WORD! His word doesn't fail. I will cry unto the God most high: unto God who performeth all things for me.

My heart was aching. My little soul chest had tumbled over. All the hurt and pain from the past was surfacing. I didn't know what to do with the emotions, that were calling out me saying, "Reckon with me, reckon with me". I sought God and he continued to assure me that he would lead and guide me.

Jeremiah 30:16-17, "I will destroy the enemy of your soul. Those things that have held you captive will be destroyed. And I the Lord will rebuild you on your ruins of your life; the things that have tried to destroy you will be destroyed!" (Living Bible).

The day came that Donnie called my spiritual mother,

my pastor's wife. The Lord had given us a scripture telling us that help was on the way. Donnie told her I was really having a hard time. Actually, I had emotionally crashed. There was a continual trail of tears and sorrow that had gripped my soul. My mother in the Lord told me, "Help is on the way". The Lord is so good to confirm his word to us. Donnie and I knew that the Holy Spirit would lead and guide us in the direction of healing.

I Was Willing

I was in a dark place. I was not eating or sleeping. The tears were constant and the memory of that terrible accident on the snowy Friday night was fresh in the forefront of my mind. My pastor's wife contacted a doctor at the Rapha Healing Center in Winston-Salem, North Carolina. I knew I needed help, so I was willing to go. That was a sad time for me. I still did not have a full understanding of why I had to walk that road, but I knew I would trust God and his guidance in my life. He had promised me that he would never leave me or forsake me. I would take him at his word. He had always been faithful!

Donnie took me to the hospital, and I signed myself in. We were both sad. We didn't understand why it was happening, but we both knew I needed Godly medical help. I was admitted and talked with the doctor. I told him what I was experiencing. He told me that the Lord had carried me all those years until I was able to face the death of my girls. I knew God had sent me to the right place. The doctor told me that I had been in a state of shock for seventeen years and when I gave my testimony, I came out of the shock state. The doctor was amazed at my testimony. He turned to

Donnie and said, "Imagine being in shock for seventeen years". He then stated that the medical field called it shock, but we knew that it was the hand of God. He had carried me through the valley of death for seventeen years and had blessed me with a good life, with the exception of the pain in my chest. I knew God used that painful experience to get inside all my hurts and pains. If we bury hurt and pain, one day that hurt and pain must be acknowledged, dug up and reckoned with, if we are going to walk in complete freedom in Christ. We must know the truth. John 8:32 states: "And ye shall know the truth and the truth shall make you free." I had found truth; the Lord had showed me through his word and through Godly men and women whom he had placed in my life for "such a time as this". The Lord wanted to heal me of all the hurt and disappointments; I had packed in my soul all those years. Now, I was willing to go through the process of identifying the problem and getting it settled, or as my pastor says "Up and Out!' God can help us bring the hurt and pain no matter what the problem might be, up and out! Not only do we want the hurt and pain up, but also out!

I began to understand what was going on with my emotions and through the doctor's direction; I was willing to let the grieving process take its course. It was a very hard thing for me to do. It was so real, and the accident had been so long ago. So many times during the grieving process, I was afraid. God would speak peace to my soul and would reassure me that he was with me. Again, I was in a place where there was no one, but God! Yes, I had Godly people and doctors who could pray and advise me, but they couldn't reach where I was standing. Nobody but God! I knew that God would bring me out.

It wasn't long before the Lord would direct me to take another step in the healing of the death of my children. As I told you, I could not recall the events of the day of my children's funeral. Grief had overwhelmed me that day. I could recall very little. The Lord gave me the scripture where Abraham buried Sara out of his sight. Genesis, 23:1-4, Verse 3, and Abraham stood up from before his dead. God was saying to me that it was time for me to stand up from the death of my girls. He wanted me to allow him to begin to apply the oil of Gideon (His healing Power) on my wounds of the grief. I had bowed down to the loss of my children long enough. It was time to take another step. Verse 3; "give me a possession of a burying place with you, that I may bury my dead out of my sight." The Lord said, "Bonnie, I want you to bury your girls out of your sight in the natural and out of the sight of your soul. I said in the natural because, I still had some of my little girls' clothes and toys. They left them in my car from the last weekend we were together. Tina, the middle child had left her little purse in the back of my car. I didn't find it until three weeks after the funeral. She had written me a letter. She had folded it perfectly. It read, "Mother, I love you, do you love me?" She had drawn two squares that said check, "yes" or "no". That was some of the hurt that I had packed many years ago that had to be put to rest, and buried out of my sight. I could not bury the memory of my precious little ones. I loved them so much, but I had to bury the hurt and the pain of losing them in that terrible accident.

Before the Lord directed me to have a private funeral. He told me in 125 days, something would happen that would be a stepping-stone for my healing. I thought, what could it be? God was saying to me that in 125 days something would occur, that will be a stepping-stone for me. Then he gave me direction about the burial. I counted the days on the calendar and it landed on Memorial Day. I did not understand what God was saying, and I knew I would have to wait until Memorial Day to find out what God was talking about.

In the meantime, I continued to question the Lord about

having the private funeral. I talked to my doctors and my spiritual leaders. I wanted to make sure that I was going in the right direction. My pastor and his wife were in constant prayer with me. Praying only that God would lead and guide me in the healing of my soul. Psalms 25:1-5, "unto you, Oh Lord, do I lift up my soul, lead me in your truths, and teach me: on you do I wait all the daylong." I knew the Lord would direct my steps.

The week before Memorial Day, I decided that I would have the private burial. I called my pastor's wife and told her about my decision. I asked her what day would be good for them, because any day was fine for Donnie and me. This is so precious. She said, "Pastor and I don't have any plans on Memorial Day, so we can do it then. I was amazed again at how direct my Father was speaking to me. I love him so much! He was there every step, and I praise him for that! He is a faithful God!

Memorial Day came and sadness still gripped my soul. I knew this day would be another day of goodbye. But, God had also promised me that it would be a stepping stone day. This was the third time since the death of my children. Three children, three funerals.

I would go to the grocery store while Donnie would make the caskets for the things I had of my girls. I made each one a spot on the bed with their pictures lying on top of their belongings and often I would go in and tell them how much I loved each one of them. That is one of the things that I hadn't done. I had not told my girls good-bye in my heart.

As I prepared to go to the grocery store, I thought that I would walk out where Donnie was preparing the caskets made from wood. Donnie began to tell me what his plans were for building them. I listened to him, and I was thinking that I wished the caskets could be different sizes. I thought that might be too much to ask, because we only had three hours before the pastor and his wife would arrive. So I told

Donnie that would be fine and off to the grocery store I went.

When I returned home, Donnie called out to me as soon as I stepped out of the car. He yelled, "Bonnie, come here! I want you to see what happened, and I didn't have anything to do with it." I said, "What?" He told me that he had cut each piece of wood the same size, and he was shocked at how they had turned out. Each box was a different size just like my girls. It was almost beyond belief for Donnie, because he knew he had cut each piece the same size. He was overwhelmed by it, but I was not. I knew God was showing me again, that I was on the right path. Psalms 94:11, "The Lord knoweth the thoughts of man." I knew God had heard the secret thoughts of my heart. He is a wonderful, faithful friend.

When the pastor and his wife arrived, we had everything prepared. I had also invited a dear couple that lived right down the street from us. Carol had been the only one outside of our spiritual leaders, which I could depend on, through this difficult time of grief. I could call on her anytime and she would come and cry with me. Carol to you I say, "Thank you!

We gathered in the room where I had their things on the bed, and my mother in the Lord led us in Amazing Grace. The pastor said, that he had sought the Lord for a word concerning this time, and he began to read from Genesis 23:1-4, the same scriptures that the Lord had given me about Abraham burying his wife Sara out of his sight. Again, God was confirming his word to me. I knew when I walked through this goodbye to my girls that it would be my stepping-stone toward my healing. I thank my God that no matter what I endured, he has been there for me, leading and guiding me in the way of righteousness.

I am thankful for a Godly husband. Donnie was heaven-sent to me. Only he could walk by my side down this road of healing. I have a wonderful husband. I know that I have already said that once, but when weighed in the balance, nothing comes up lacking. He is a faithful husband, and I love him with all my heart. Chezz my son was so understanding, he is another gift from God. He was always saying to me, "You're going to be alright mother. I thank God for a beautiful family that serves, "The Living God". "The God of the Bible is the God of our home. Psalms 127:1, "Except the Lord builds a house, they labor in vain that built it."

After the funeral, I knew it was going to be easier. Now, I had said the goodbye that I needed so much to say. I thank the Lord for ordering my steps by his word. Psalms 119:133, "Order my steps in thy word: and let not iniquity have dominion over me." I believe that as I kept my mind on God, and desired his word even in the hardest time of my life, he has showed himself faithful. I'm amazed, that the same God, who delivered the Hebrew children out of the fiery furnace, delivered me from death so many times. I just love the Lord so much. He is the Lord of Heaven and Earth, and my praise shall always be unto him.

Two years went by, the grieving times still came and went, but I knew how to release it and not pack it. It really feels good to be able to cry. The Lord again led me down the road of wholeness. He led me to a doctor with Cross Life Ministries. It was counseling and teaching with the mind of Christ. Through this doctor, the Lord began to teach me how he could heal my memory. My doctor and counselor gave me the word of God with each visit. The word of God became my healing oil and I would apply it to each painful memory. As I obeyed the word of God, I would see the healing "Hand of God", concerning the painful memory of the past. For seventeen years, I only had bad memories of my little girls, and every time those memories surfaced, I would quickly pack them down into my little soul chest. The good days that my girls and I shared were not attainable in my mind. I tried so many times in those seventeen years to find the good days and the good times, but the bad always stood guard at the door of my memory. With God's word came understanding. I realized that God could go back to that terrible night, and touch my memory and heal me of those painful, painful memories. I was open again for God to do what he had to do. Do what you need to do God! I didn't understand everything that God was doing in me, but I acknowledged that only He could go back there, because He is the God of my yesterdays, today and forevermore.

One night lying in my bed something like a camera flash crossed in my mind, and suddenly I could see my girls,' faces, each face with a big grin on it. I cried tears of joy. There were my memories of the good times we'd had. As days went by, I remembered more and more of the happy times. Instead of looking back, I was looking forward with excitement to that Blessed Day when we would be united, never to part again.

The Lord, through his word, showed me from Corinthians 13:11 that he now wanted to heal that little girl in me. This again would be a stepping-stone for me. Paul said, "When I was a child, I spake as a child, I thought as a child, I understood as a child: but when I became a man I put away childish things." The Lord began showing me the little girl in me that had never been put away. God showed me that the child would rule and control my destiny with her rejection and hurts. So again, I was open for God to do whatever needed to get rid of the child in me. The Holy Spirit would shine his light on this little girl attitude each time she would show her presence. It was up to me to put her away, and I was diligent to obey the direction of the Holy Spirit.

I realized this little girl was the little girl, who was hurt long ago, and she still remembered the pain and hurt she had endured. I must put her away or, root the child out of me.

The Lord is so gracious to help me to see my faults. I thank him so much for his eye that kept watch over me. HE IS A FAITHFUL GOD!

∞

As I turn and look down the road that I have walked, I am in awe of God. He has carried me through this journey of life that has been laid out before me. I give him all the glory for his marvelous love, care and work in my life. Glory be to God!

He is still working on me. I have not arrived yet, but I'm further today than yesterday, and I have faith that he will continue to teach me his ways and show me his paths.

Psalm 25:4,5, "Show me thy ways, O Lord; teach me thy ways. Lead me in thy truth, and teach me: for thy art the God of my salvation; on thee do I wait all the day."

He is the God of my salvation and his word is truth, and he loves you and me more than we could ever comprehend. I can't say that enough. He is Faithful!

I pray this testimony of God's faithfulness in my life has touched you. I pray for those suffering from the past, that you will let the God of your yesterday heal your hurts and pain. I pray that you have realized that the God of our today is the God of our yesterdays. He can and will walk with you back to that time of pain and hurt, and heal and deliver your soul from the past so you can go forward.

Isaiah 61:1-3, "The spirit of the Lord God is upon me, because the Lord has anointed me to bring good news to the suffering and afflicted. He has sent me to comfort the broken-hearted, to announce liberty to captives and to open the eyes of the blind. He has sent me to tell those who mourn that the time of God's favor to them has come, and the day of his wrath to their enemies.

> Beauty for ashes:
> Joy instead of mourning:
> Praise instead of heaviness:
> For God has planted then like strong and
> graceful oaks for his glory."

To God Be The Glory!

Biography

Believing the call on her life according to Ephesians 4:12, is to teach the word of God for the perfecting of the saints. This is the desire that God has placed in her heart to reach out to the body of Christ. Bonnie has received powerful truths from the word of God through revelation of the Holy Spirit that will set the captives free and cause them to walk in the abundance of the finished work of the cross. Bonnie believes that when the body of Christ receives revelation knowledge of the word of God it enables the believer to walk in perfect liberty.

Bonnie has taught on "Leaving the Past Behind, "Healing Damaged Emotions, "and the "Prosperity of God in the Lives of the Saints, "and many other topics. Bonnie has completed her first book entitled, "The Heart of a Mother and the Hand of God" which is soon to be released.

Bonnie Horton has been a born again Christian since 1980. She has been teaching the word of God since 1986. She is currently enrolled in the Christian Life School of Theology in which she has earned an Associate Degree. Bonnie is a local church minister of the PHC of the South Carolina Conference, located in Lake City South Carolina.

Bonnie is a Native American and resides in Laurinburg, North Carolina with her husband and partner in ministry. Bonnie has been married to Donnie Horton for 22 years and they have one precious son, Chezz Horton. They are members of Northview Harvest Ministries where Bonnie also ministers.

Testimony of Bonnie Horton

It was the year 1979, when I suffered the loss of my three children due to a tragic automobile accident. It was a snowy Friday evening, and my children were passengers in a car that lost control and slid into an icy river. The automobile was submerged and my children tragically lost their lives. My girls were nine, seven and three at the time of the accident. I became engulfed in such immense grief and sorrow and saw no way of escape. I only wanted to die. I couldn't imagine life without my girls. How could I go on? Why should I go on? There was no hope.I was a dead woman.

After the funeral services were held, I planned how I would take my life, as soon I could be alone. Life had no meaning for me and my desire was to die. At that moment, life without my children made Hell look easy. At 7:00 a.m. the next morning, five minutes before I was about to take a bottle of sleeping pills, a knock came at my grandmother's door. It was a missionary who said she needed to see me right away. She told me that God had sent her to me. She told me about Jesus and how he could turn my life around. As she was telling me about Jesus, I was thinking in my mind, "Lady you don't know what I am dealing with and you don't know how I hurt". She continued to tell about the love of God and what a difference he could make in my life. Having been raised in a Christian home, I knew about God but had never experienced God. As she ministered to me in my mind I was thinking, O.K God I know that the Bible says you are the God who split the Red Sea, and you are the God who delivered Daniel from the lions den, and you are the God who raised Lazarus from the Dead and if you can do anything for me at this time in my life you have to prove yourself right now. I gave God an option, show me your power now or I die. I was at a crossroad and I knew death's door was open just waiting for me to enter. She led me in the sinner's prayer and immediately when I asked the Lord Jesus Christ into my heart and repented of my sins, God with his mighty hand picked me up. All the grief, all the sorrow and all the hurt took wings and flew.

Since the day I gave my heart to the Lord he has held my hand through life. Everything the enemy meant for bad the Lord and turned around for good. I have been blessed with a wonderful husband and son. God has and always had a purpose and plan for my life. Through the tragedy suffered, God has placed a desire within me to reach out to others who are suffering from the past and walking in darkness. The divine call upon my life is to teach and preach that there is abundant life through the love of Jesus Christ.

If you would like to write the author
Or
Schedule her to speak
She can be contacted through:

Bonnie Horton

Streams of Living Water Ministries
P.O Box 4435 Oak Grove Rd.
Laurinburg, North Carolina 28352
(910) 276 6770—e-mail bonniesministry@earthlink.com
Web page: bonniehorton.com

Printed in the United States
17282LVS00002B/772-819